Waddle I Do without You?

MICHELLE SCHUSTERMAN

Waddle I Do without You?

Scholastic Inc.

For Rosa

Copyright © 2023 by Michelle Schusterman

All rights reserved. Published by Scholastic Inc., *Publishers since 1920.* SCHOLASTIC and associated logos are trademarks and/or registered trademarks of Scholastic Inc.

The publisher does not have any control over and does not assume any responsibility for author or third-party websites or their content.

No part of this publication may be reproduced, stored in a retrieval system, or transmitted in any form or by any means, electronic, mechanical, photocopying, recording, or otherwise, without written permission of the publisher. For information regarding permission, write to Scholastic Inc., Attention: Permissions Department, 557 Broadway, New York, NY 10012.

This book is a work of fiction. Names, characters, places, and incidents are either the product of the author's imagination or are used fictitiously, and any resemblance to actual persons, living or dead, business establishments, events, or locales is entirely coincidental.

ISBN 978-1-338-89325-0

10 9 8 7 6 5 4 3 2 1   23 24 25 26 27

Printed in the U.S.A.   40

First printing 2023

Book design by Omou Barry

Interior icons © Shutterstock.com

1

ADDIE

"Max! Where'd you go, my noble steed?"

Addie hurried down the beach, her sparkly jewel-studded leather riding boots sinking into the soft sand. To her right, the crystal clear waters of the Indian Ocean stretched on and on, the foamy tide lapping almost all the way to her feet. To her left, scraggly green bushes stretched all the way up to the woods in the distance. Addie slowed her pace and squinted, scanning the bushes for any sign of sprites—those clever little fairies with hypnotic eyes and translucent wings were always lurking around close to sunset, waiting for a chance to cause mischief. Maybe there were a few hiding in that rickety old rowboat?

Then she spotted a gray-and-white tail sticking out

of the bramble like an extremely fluffy shark fin. It wagged the moment she saw it, and Addie giggled.

The spell was broken.

"Okay, Max," she called, making her way carefully through the brush. Tiny stickers clung to her dingy sneakers. They weren't made of leather, and they weren't boots, but Addie had sewn a couple of fake rhinestones on top, so they did sparkle a little. "We need to head back home. It's going to get dark soon! Besides, we might run into a sprite out here."

Max let out a little whine.

"I know, I know," Addie said with a sigh. "There are no sprites. That we know of, anyway."

Max lifted his shaggy head and gave a short, loud bark. Then he stuck his nose back into the brush.

"Did you find a stick?" Addie glanced at her phone. If they were even just a few minutes late, Dad would be super worried. "We don't have time for fetch, Max!"

Max barked again. He didn't budge, and Addie's smile faded.

He hadn't just found a particularly good stick. This was something important he wanted her to come take a look at. Addie didn't hesitate. She stuffed her phone in her pocket and made her way through the brush.

When Addie reached Max, he lowered his head and sniffed at something. He looked up again, and Addie gasped.

"A sea turtle!" she said, kneeling down carefully and reaching out to stroke the tiny turtle's shell. "Oh, this is even cooler than a sprite. He's just a baby, Max," she said, smiling. The turtle was only a little bit bigger than the palm of Addie's hand, but she knew sea turtles could grow to be enormous. Even more enormous than Max, and he weighed over a hundred pounds!

The baby turtle lifted his head and gazed dolefully at Addie. "You've got a long way back to the water, little guy," Addie whispered, touching the top of the baby turtle's head. "Want some help getting home?"

The turtle didn't respond, obviously. But Addie often had conversations with all kinds of animals and sea creatures in her head. She imagined this baby turtle was saying, *Yes, please. I'd like to be back in the water before the sun sets or my mother will scold me.*

Addie carefully picked the baby turtle up with both hands. Max led the way out of the bushes, and the two of them strolled down the beach toward the water. The sun was already halfway below the horizon. Addie thought it looked like a glowing red orb that was gently warming the baby turtle's bathwater.

When the water crept up to her shoes, Addie stopped and crouched. "Here you go, little guy," she said, touching the turtle's head one last time before setting him gently in the shallow water. "Hope you don't get in trouble with your mom!"

The baby turtle crawled forward. A few seconds later, the water gently lifted him up. Addie couldn't help but laugh at the way his limbs flailed as the current carried him back out into the ocean.

But then a few seconds later, the water delivered him right back to Addie's feet.

"Uh-oh." Addie leaned over and scooped the turtle up again. She moved out a little farther, then tried to release him again. And again. And *again*.

Each time, the current just brought the baby turtle right back to land.

"He's too light," Addie told Max, picking up the turtle and looking around. "I need to get him farther out there. Hmm . . ."

Her gaze fell on the rickety old rowboat.

Never, ever go out in a boat alone! Addie had heard Dad say it at least a thousand times. It was his number one rule—and he had *lots* of rules. But Addie's feet were already moving toward the rowboat, and then she was dragging it toward the water, and then she was climbing inside with the turtle.

Max barked sharply at her as the boat drifted away from the coast. "It's fine, Max!" Addie called, picking up the oars. "I'll be right back!"

It wasn't like she was going out to sea. Not the way Dad did when he went fishing.

"Here's a good spot," Addie said, picking up the baby turtle. "Off you go!"

She lowered her hands into the water. The baby turtle wiggled his limbs, then took off swimming with a speed that surprised Addie. She laughed as he disappeared into the deep blue water.

Was it weird that she felt a little bit jealous of the

turtle? Imagine having the whole entire ocean as your home! Addie loved snorkeling. She was constantly amazed at the beautiful world that existed below the surface. The coast of Australia where she lived was home to a ton of unique wildlife, and she couldn't get enough of it. Every creature, from sea dragons to koalas, totally fascinated her.

And they were everywhere! Anytime Addie and Max took a walk, they met a new creature. The little house where they lived with Dad was right on the coast. Even though the city of Perth was only a fifteen-minute drive away, there were hardly any people out here.

"Arf! *Arf!*"

Max's distant bark startled Addie. How long had she been sitting here while the boat drifted farther out in the water? She grabbed the oars and began rowing back to shore. But every time the boat got close to the sand, the current would pull her back out a few feet.

Finally, Addie tossed down the oars and sighed. "Sorry, shoes," she said, swinging one leg over the side of the boat and wincing at the chill of the water. It was almost waist-deep, and by the time Addie dragged the boat back onto the beach, her jeans and shoes were soaked through.

Max nuzzled Addie's hand with his big wet nose, and she suddenly realized the sun was about to slip below the horizon. "Uh-oh. Dad!"

Together, Addie and Max began to run. Or rather, Addie jogged as fast as she could, with her sneakers squelching in the sand, while Max loped along easily at her side.

The coast curved gently up to the north, and Addie made sure to stay just close enough to the water so that Dad would be able to see her and Max coming from the kitchen window. Dad could be kind of a worrywart sometimes, especially when Addie lost track of time when she was outside exploring.

Last year, Addie had been at their neighbor Mrs. Miller's house while Dad was at his trivia night. She'd been in the yard playing with Mrs. Miller's chickens when she spotted a possum—*flying!* Addie had raced into the trees after the amazing creature, which she was pretty sure was called a sugar glider.

She hadn't found it. And okay, she'd ended up

getting a little bit lost for a few hours. But Max had found her, hadn't he? So really, Dad grounding her for a week had been an overreaction.

Max was twelve years old, just like she was. Dad had adopted Max right after Addie was born, and before her mom passed away. He had tons of photos of tiny baby Addie curled up in her crib next to the world's shaggiest gray-and-white puppy.

"This walk turned out to be a rescue mission!" Addie told Max cheerfully, huffing and puffing as she jogged. "Not that the baby turtle needed rescuing. I'm sure he would've made it to the water eventually. But boy, I bet his mom wouldn't have been happy if it was after dark!"

Max's tongue lolled out the side of his mouth.

"Yeah, yeah, I know," Addie said, picking up speed. "Dad's not going to be happy either if we don't hurry!"

Addie could just make out their one-story house painted a cheery yellow, with a little boathouse not far behind it. Sometimes, when she was in the distance like this, Addie pretended she lived in a fairy-tale cottage, only instead of being in a mysterious forest that might have witches who lurked in candy houses or trolls that hid under bridges, her cottage was surrounded by Australia's most magical wildlife. And as the hero of the fairy tale, Addie could speak all their languages.

Dad bought their house way before Addie was born. As a fisherman, he wanted a quiet little part of the beach where he could take his boat out and the fish wouldn't be disturbed by tourists or surfers. This was the only home she had ever had, and she loved it. The best part? There was a little island right off the coast that was the home of the littlest species of penguins in the world—blue penguins, also called fairy penguins.

So really, it wasn't hard for Addie to imagine she lived in a fairy tale!

Even so, she got lonely every once in a while, especially when Dad was out fishing. Addie was homeschooled, so she spent a lot of time with Max napping at her feet while she wrote essays and finished her math worksheets. Still, even fairy-tale heroes liked to hang out with actual kids sometimes.

A few months ago, Dad had signed her up for a

youth environmental group called Eco-Guardians. They met every Saturday to talk about local environmental causes and explore all the wildlife around Perth. It was definitely the best birthday gift ever!

"Did I tell you we're going to the Leda Nature Reserve this weekend?" Addie told Max. He snorted once, which meant, *Yes, a hundred times.* "It's going to be a pretty long hike, boy. You're going to have to rest up!"

Max gave her what was decidedly a very derisive look. Addie grinned. When Max was a puppy, he had even more energy than she did! Walks like this were more like runs, with her struggling to keep up with his constant pouncing from one place to the next, stopping to sniff only for a few seconds before charging out into the waves, then tearing back toward her, sopping wet, with seaweed clinging to his thick fur.

Now Addie was the one sopping wet. She wished she could give herself a good shake the way Max did, but that probably wouldn't dry off her jeans.

Addie's phone buzzed in her pocket (thank goodness for waterproof phone cases), and she pulled it out eagerly. She usually lost reception on these walks, but

now that she was getting closer to the house a few notifications had popped up.

"It's Bree!" she exclaimed, opening the messages
app. Bree and Jake were Addie's two best friends from
Eco-Guardians.

Bree

> You guys want to come over after the hike on
> Saturday? Movie night!

Addie slowed her pace a little, but Max kept going.
As she was typing, Jake responded with three thumbs-
up emojis. Addie bounced up and down a little as she
hit send.

Addie

> Yes please! Just let me check with my dad.

Bree

> Cool!

Addie shoved her phone in her pocket and broke
into a run, following Max all the way to the house.
She waved at Dad, who stood at the kitchen window,
and he waved back. Addie breathed a sigh of relief as

she slowed down a little. She'd made it home in time—barely.

But she still had to change out of her wet clothes before Dad saw. She didn't want to risk getting in trouble, especially when she had to ask Dad about movie night.

Addie knew that he would want to call Bree's parents first since he'd never met them before. But once he talked to them, he was bound to say yes. Right?

Addie tried not to feel impatient as she hurried up the porch steps after Max. Dad hadn't said no yet! But she couldn't help thinking about how Jake had responded right away. He probably hadn't even had to ask for permission. Meanwhile, Dad still asked Mrs. Miller to come over and babysit anytime he went out at night. Addie was pretty positive Bree and Jake didn't need babysitters anymore.

Inside, Addie breathed in a rich familiar aroma. She kicked off her soggy shoes by the door as Max trotted over to his water bowl and began to lap messily, splashing flicks all over the little rug under the bowl. When he was a puppy, Max would "dig" in his water with his big paws, causing a mini tsunami every time. He hadn't done that in a long time, but they still kept the rug there just in case.

Taking a deep breath, Addie tried to tiptoe past the kitchen to her room.

"Addie?"

Dad poked his head out of the kitchen, and Addie froze. She spun around and smiled brightly. "Hi!"

"Dinner's just about ready!"

Addie followed Dad into the kitchen, where a stockpot was bubbling merrily on the stove. Dad was fresh out of the shower and already wearing his pajamas, his brown hair wet and messy. Addie knew he'd be out like a light right after dinner, since he woke up when it was still dark to take the boat out on the water.

"Is that ham and pea soup?" Addie asked eagerly, peering into the pot.

"I had tons of peas left over from our last market trip," Dad explained, taking out his earbuds and slipping them into his pocket. "I figure the weather is only going to get warmer from here, might as well have soup while we still can!"

"Yum!" Addie began to set the little table with two bowls, two spoons, and two napkins. She opened her mouth to tell Dad about Bree's text, but then—

"How was the walk?" Dad asked. Then he frowned. "Why are your jeans so wet?"

"So . . . funny story!" Addie said lightly as Max ambled into the kitchen. "Max found a baby sea turtle."

Max sat next to the pantry door where they kept his food and gave her an expectant look. *It's dinner time for all of us, Addie.* That was what that look meant.

Dad was smiling. "A baby sea turtle, really?"

"Yeah! In the brush. We helped him get back to the water. It was so cute!"

Addie opened the pantry door and pulled out the plastic container, scooping two heaps of food into Max's bowl. Once Max was chomping down happily, Addie turned back to find Dad looking at her expectantly.

"But how did you get so wet?"

Addie shrugged. "Oh, well, the current kept carrying the turtle back in, so I had to go out a little farther."

Dad looked amused. "You waded out up to your waist?"

Yes, Addie tried to say. But she couldn't. Addie sometimes thought maybe a witch had cursed her as a baby so that she could never tell a lie—at least not to Dad. She always ended up blurting out the truth.

"I took that old rowboat out just far enough to let the turtle go and I rowed back to the shore just fine but I couldn't get close enough to the sand so I had to jump out and drag the boat back and everything turned out *fine!*"

Dad's smile faded. "Addie. You took a boat out alone?"

Addie winced. "Barely! It wasn't that far."

"You know the rule." Dad's brow furrowed as he stirred the soup. "Being out on the water can be unpredictable. Even close to shore. Did you stop and think before you got in that boat?"

Stop and think. Dad was always encouraging Addie to do that. She chewed her lip nervously. "I *thought,*" she told him. "But I didn't *stop.* The baby turtle needed help—it was an emergency!"

"And what's the rule about emergencies?" Dad asked.

Addie hung her head. "Call you?"

"Right."

"I'm sorry," Addie said, and she meant it. Now that she thought about it, Dad could have helped her make sure the baby turtle got back home. But in the moment, Addie just wanted to fix the problem *now*.

"It's okay," Dad said, turning back to the soup. "Just remember for next time."

"Okay." Addie paused. "So you know how Eco-Guardians have that hike on Saturday?"

Dad chuckled. "At the reserve? Yes, honey. You've only mentioned it about a hundred times this week."

"Well, Bree just texted and asked if maybe I could come watch a movie at her house after."

"That sounds fun," Dad said, turning off the stove. "Can you get her parents' phone number for me so I can have a chat with them first?" He turned and caught her mouthing the words along with him. Addie winced, but Dad just chuckled. "I didn't say no, honey.

I just want to get to know your new friend's parents first, okay?"

Addie nodded. "Yeah. No problem."

She pulled out what was left of the bread they'd gotten from the market last weekend and began to cut a few thick slices. As she did, her phone buzzed again, and she slipped it out of her pocket. This time, it was a TikTok notification.

Bree and Jake both loved TikTok and uploaded videos a few times a day. They convinced Addie to make an account, but hardly anyone had watched the few videos she'd posted of the beach. Jake's videos were usually a lot of goofy dances that he made up, or videos of the dogs at the animal shelter in Perth where he volunteered. Bree's videos were usually all about climate change and tips on how to be less wasteful— but she always delivered them in silly voices that made Addie laugh so hard she would have to watch the video five times just to catch all of it.

This notification was a new video Jake had shared, and Addie giggled as she watched him and Bree dancing while waiting in line at the corner store near their school. Another kid joined in, then another, and even the shop owner joined in as he rang up Jake's bag of Cheezels!

Addie paused to hear the video, then got back to slicing the bread. The video made her smile, but it also made her feel kind of left out. Bree and Jake were in each other's videos a lot because they would film them during lunch or at recess. When they first found out that Addie was homeschooled, they thought it was awesome.

"You can sleep as late as you want!" Jake said, shaking his head in awe.

Bree had gestured to her green-and-blue checkered skirt. "Forget sleep. You don't have to wear a uniform! I'm so jealous."

And in a lot of ways, Addie agreed. She could take long breaks from schoolwork and go for a walk on the beach and explore. Plus, Dad was a really great teacher.

But she couldn't help feeling jealous, too. Jealous that Bree and Jake got to see each other and all their other friends every single day while Addie was always just counting down the hours until Saturday.

As if he'd read her mind, Max came up and nuzzled her hand again. Smiling, Addie tore off a tiny piece of bread and tossed it to him.

"You're right, boy. I get to hang out with you every day," she said softly, scratching Max behind the ears.

But she couldn't help wishing she could see her other friends more often, too. Watching her friends' videos made her feel like a lonely princess locked in a tower—only Addie's hair wasn't anywhere near long enough to climb down and escape.

2
MAX

Max had an *excellent* vocabulary. *Amazing. Bonza. Totally epic*, which was one of Addie's favorite phrases.

"Max, that was totally epic!" Addie said just last week at the dog park in Perth when Max made an admittedly impressive Frisbee catch. Max loved the dog park, where people were always exclaiming over his size or his long, shaggy fur, not to mention giving him lots of belly rubs. Plus, there were always a million new things to sniff. There were also lots of dogs getting trained—usually puppies, but sometimes dogs who were old enough that they really should know better—and Max always felt a little sad when they struggled.

"Sit! Come on, Ghost! *Sit!*" a young boy with a

round, freckled face begged his tiny white pit bull puppy, who just gazed up at him lovingly.

Finally, Max trotted over and plopped his butt down on the ground right next to Ghost. "Like this," he said.

"Oh!" Ghost mimicked the move, and the boy beamed.

"Good girl!" the boy said. "Lie down?"

Max instantly lowered all the way down on the grass, and so did Ghost. Addie and Dad came over to watch as the boy continued training Ghost—or rather, as *Max* continued training Ghost. By the time Max left, Ghost had learned *stay, come, leave it,* and *drop it.*

"You're the master, Max," Addie said proudly.

Dad chuckled. "No one would ever guess how long it took to teach him *stay.*"

Max remembered how challenging *stay* was at first. Not because he didn't understand pretty quickly what Dad or Addie wanted him to do, but because he was exploding with puppy energy. He'd learned how to control himself, though. Most of the time, anyway.

And Max's learning hadn't stopped there. Because

Addie said a *lot* of words. Of course, it hadn't been that way for the first few years. Max had been full-grown way before Addie, and for a few years her vocabulary was just about the right size for him. Then she had started learning words at a pace that almost overwhelmed him, and every day there was just a stream of words coming out and he had no idea what any of them meant. So he made it a point to listen. To memorize. Addie told everyone that Max understood every word she said, and Max was going to make sure that was true.

"Tomorrow's Thursday," Dad said, dunking a slice of bread in his soup. Max lay down next to the table, hoping for a stray piece of ham. "Trivia night."

"What's the theme for the trivia?" Addie asked. Max's ears twitched. He wasn't sure what *theme* meant, but he was more interested in the tone of her voice. It had that slightly sly quality that he learned long ago meant she was thinking something a little bit different than what she was saying.

"Action films of the nineties," Dad said, pumping his fist. "I'm going to dominate."

Addie giggled and then cleared her throat. "You're always home from trivia night by ten. Maybe this time, me and Max can just stay on our own? No babysitter?"

Babysitter. That was a word Max knew well. It meant that Dad was going to be out at night and Mrs. Miller was going to come over and sit in the recliner and watch shows and make popcorn, which was great in Max's opinion because she was very generous.

But apparently Addie didn't feel the same way. That also took Max a little while to figure out. Because Addie liked Mrs. Miller just fine. Then he'd realized Addie wanted to stay home by herself. Well, not by herself. With Max. And Dad didn't want Addie home alone without a grown-up.

Dad sighed. "Addie, we've talked about this. Not till high school. Mrs. Miller will be here around seven, and I told her there would be lots of leftover soup for dinner."

"Don't you think that Mrs. Miller has better things to do than sit around with a twelve-year-old girl who's perfectly capable of taking care of herself?" Addie asked.

"Addie, haven't we had this conversation? I know you're capable. But you're also impulsive."

Impulsive. Max had been waiting for that word to come up. He'd been proud when he'd finally figured out what it meant. *Impulsive* meant that Addie sometimes didn't think things through. But it was okay because Max was always there to rescue her.

Like the time she'd chased that flying possum into the woods behind Mrs. Miller's house, and Max had followed her scent to find her.

Or the time Addie leaned over the side of Dad's boat because she thought she saw a stingray, and Max snatched the hem of her shirt with his teeth as the boat hit a wave so she wouldn't fall out.

Or just now, on their walk! Max had watched anxiously as Addie's boat drifted farther and farther out to sea after she'd released the turtle. She'd been totally lost in thought, which happened a lot. Max's bark had gotten her attention before she sailed out too far.

"I *swear* I won't do anything impulsive," Addie pleaded. "Come on, I don't need a babysitter, Dad!"

But she does *need me,* Max thought. *I'm her guardian*.

Addie was adventurous and loved to explore, and Max had lost count of the number of times she'd stumbled and skinned her knees, or pricked her finger on a plant she was overly curious about, or got a little too close to an animal or sea creature that Max knew instinctively did not want a little girl anywhere near it.

Max loved Addie, but he had to agree with Dad on this one. She was *very* impulsive.

Dad rubbed his eyes and shook his head. "Addie, I've already called Mrs. Miller. Let's circle back to this when you're a little older."

Addie groaned. "That's what you always say."

Dad and Addie continued talking about babysitters, but a distant rumbling caught Max's attention and he tuned them out. The fur on the back of his neck prickled and he tensed, unable to stop the low growl emitting from his throat.

Addie glanced down at him. "What's the matter, boy?" she asked, frowning slightly. Dad stood up and walked to the window over the kitchen sink, peering outside.

"Looks like a little bit of lightning way out there over the water," he said. "I don't think it's supposed to storm tonight, though."

Storm.

Max's least favorite word in all the hundreds of words that he knew.

Addie pulled out her phone. "Yeah, it's not going to come anywhere near us tonight. Don't worry, Max. I'm sure the thundering will stop soon."

Max relaxed slightly, resting his head on his paws. *Stop soon* was another phrase he knew. If Addie said the storm was going to *stop soon*, that meant everything was going to be okay.

He dozed off a little bit while Addie and Dad cleaned the dishes. It was only when he heard Addie's footsteps leaving the kitchen that Max stood up and shook himself off. He never used to have to take naps before bedtime, but it was happening more and more lately. Addie teased him about it a lot.

He padded into her room after her, where Addie

was already sprawled on her bed and scrolling on her phone. Soon she was giggling, and music was blasting from the little speaker on her phone. Max was just about to hop up on the bed with her when he heard the distant thunder rumble again. And even though it was far away, to his embarrassment, he tucked his tail between his legs and shrank over to the corner of the room.

"Oh, Max! It's okay!" Addie hopped off the bed, tossing her phone aside. She hurried into her closet and rummaged around, then appeared a moment later holding a familiar stuffed kangaroo. "Look what Dad found when he was cleaning out the garage yesterday. Do you remember Roo?"

She held the brown-and-black kangaroo, which was missing one ear, out for Max to sniff. A flood of memories rushed through him, and his tail flopped once on the carpet. Roo had been his favorite toy as a puppy. He carried it everywhere, chewing on it in a loving way, never really intending to destroy it (the ear had been an accident). Roo had always given him comfort. Even though he was still anxious, he felt himself relax a little, and Addie tucked Roo at his side.

"You're still just a puppy sometimes, aren't you, Max?" she said fondly, planting a kiss right between his eyes. But as Addie hopped back up on the bed and picked up her phone, Max felt ashamed. He wasn't a puppy. He was a grown dog, and Addie's guardian. Deliberately leaving Roo behind, Max plodded over to the beanbag Addie kept by the window and sprawled across it. He could still sense the storm, and it made his fur prickle.

Stop soon, he told himself. *Stop soon, stop soon.*

Max repeated it over and over again until he drifted off to sleep.

3
DARWIN

Darwin was a blue penguin. But he didn't always feel like one.

Sometimes he felt like a shark. They were clever and focused, like Darwin when he hunted krill along the ocean floor. (Although Darwin wasn't really the best hunter.)

Sometimes he felt like a swan. They moved so gracefully, like Darwin when he swam at top speed through the water, rising and falling with the currents. (But on land, Darwin wasn't graceful at all.)

Sometimes he felt like a squid. They were always alone, unlike a school of fish or a herd of sea lions . . . or a colony of penguins.

Technically, Darwin was part of a colony. But right now, he was on a solo dive. He flattened his wings to his sides as he sped down, down, down like a shark, then twisted around and soared up, up, up until he broke the surface and glided toward the island like a swan.

Then he clambered over the rocks and came to a halt in front of several penguins, who looked at him like he was a squid.

Dubbo turned away slightly. Kurri lifted her beak up to the sky. Junee stared down at her webbed feet. And Tam looked right at Darwin, but she didn't tilt her head.

Darwin had figured that one out pretty recently, and he was proud of himself. When Tam saw a penguin and tilted her head, that meant she was happy to see them. She almost never tilted her head when she saw Darwin.

"Darwin!" Tam said sharply. "Were you on a solo dive?"

"Yes," Darwin replied.

"It's too dangerous to do that all on your own,

Darwin!" she exclaimed. "There are sea lions out there!"

This made no sense to Darwin. "There are sea lions out there when we hunt in groups," he pointed out. But for some reason, that just made Tam roll her eyes.

"Safety in numbers," she said. "You know the rule, Darwin. You're so impulsive!"

It was just another rule of the penguin colony that Darwin knew but didn't understand. It was like the whole colony shared one mind and they always knew exactly what one another was thinking. And then Darwin had his own solo mind, and it wasn't connected to theirs at all.

Which didn't bother him, not usually. He liked how his mind worked. Darwin was the smallest penguin in the colony, and he might have been the last one his age to learn how to swim or catch krill, and yes, he was definitely, without a doubt, the worst diver around. But he was very, very clever.

It was just that he had a hard time communicating his great ideas to the other penguins, and so they didn't realize how clever he was.

"Are you all going on a dive right now?" Darwin asked just as his stomach gave a loud rumble. "Can I come?"

"Didn't you catch anything on your solo dive?" Dubbo asked.

"No," Darwin admitted.

Tam sighed. "I'd be happy to bring you back a krill or two, Darwin. You don't have to come."

Darwin didn't respond for a second, because he was stuck on the word *happy*. He knew what happy meant. But Tam wasn't happy. Tam hadn't tilted her head.

"I want to come," he replied. And when the other penguins didn't respond, he tried tilting his head to make it more *happy*. "I want to come!"

Dubbo flapped his wings. He did that a lot. It meant he was annoyed. "You aren't the best diver, Darwin. You're going to slow us down."

Darwin liked Dubbo a lot. Because Dubbo was very honest. He always said exactly what he was thinking, and Darwin appreciated that.

"I'm not the best diver," Darwin agreed. "I'm the

worst diver! And that's why I need to practice. Also, I've been thinking about it, and I have a better strategy for us to hunt! Instead of spreading out and then going deep, I think we should spread out more up and down."

Junee looked directly at him now. "Spread out up and down? I don't understand what that means."

Darwin was thrilled to be taken seriously for once. "It means that—"

But then Tam interrupted. "We already have a strategy, and this is not the time to try a new one. We dive, everyone knows their direction, and then after we spread out, we go deep. Ready?"

"Ready!" all the other penguins chorused instantly, except Darwin. When Tam shot him a look, he nodded.

But he couldn't bring himself to say *ready*. Because he wasn't ready. He had a better strategy, and he really wanted to try it.

The others turned at the same moment and waddled toward the edge of the short cliff on the western point of the island. Darwin hurried to keep up. He could hear the splashes as one by one the others dove into the waves. Darwin was the last to dive in, and it was only when he was under the water that he realized he wasn't sure what direction he was supposed to go in. Because he'd showed up to the meeting late, and Tam hadn't told him.

The others were already out of sight. So Darwin just started going deep.

The water was aqua, then blue, then nearly black. Darwin loved all the layers of the sea. When he was on land, he felt a little bit clunky and a little bit slow. But even though he was the worst diver in the colony, he still loved diving. He loved swimming, too. He just swam in a different way. While the other penguins were graceful, moving in a smooth line that cut straight through the water, Darwin loved to twist and turn. Maybe he could swim a little faster if he went straight like they did, but there was a benefit to Darwin's way, too. He could constantly see what was around him, making sure there were no predators, and making sure he didn't pass by any delicious opportunities for a snack. Darwin twisted and turned, deeper and deeper, and before long he started to hear the other penguins call out to one another.

"This way!" shouted Tam.

"This way!" cried Kurri.

"This way!" yelled Junee.

They were all above him, but in different directions. After a moment, he heard Dubbo, too. "This way!"

"That way!" Darwin called, amused with himself.

No one responded.

Darwin enjoyed his hunting time, even though there were no fish in sight. A few dozen other penguins joined the hunting party. When Darwin was down deep, he could see all of them above him, soaring around in an ever-changing pattern. Every time Darwin thought he saw the pattern, it changed—and as clever as he was, he couldn't figure out how he fit into it.

So as usual, he didn't try.

Soon, he started to hear the others call out: "Got one! Got one!" Darwin thought about what Tam had said about bringing him back some krill. He was going to find his own this time, no matter what!

Suddenly, Kurri called out, *"Hear!"*

Darwin was confused. "I can hear you!" he called back, but Kurri didn't respond.

He could sense the other penguins immediately switching directions, calling out as they made their way close to Kurri. Why were they all going to the same place? It wasn't like they could all share a krill!

That's when Darwin spotted something far above him. A jellyfish! He soared upward, twisting and turning and making his way toward the tasty creature.

"Stop!"

"Stop!"

"Stop!"

"Stop!"

That wasn't a signal Darwin had ever heard. But he could tell it was directed at him. The others were cheering him on as he made his catch! He clamped down on the jellyfish and swallowed it whole, and suddenly there was a flurry of movement as a giant school of krill just above the jellyfish swam off at top speed.

Darwin made his way to the surface, his stomach nice and full. He had never seen a school of krill that up close before! They had been moving together so tightly, they almost looked like one big creature. Kind of like how he felt the colony moved without him.

When he reached the surface, the other penguins were already swimming their way toward the coast. Darwin waddled out and shook himself dry, fully expecting wild applause. But all the other penguins were glaring at him, and he tried tilting his head.

"Happy?" he asked.

Tam shook her head. "No, we're not happy! Darwin, you messed up our whole strategy! We were supposed to surround the school of krill. We could've brought back so much krill for the rest of the colony! What were you thinking?"

"I . . . I saw a jellyfish," Darwin explained. "I didn't see the school of krill."

"Didn't you hear Kurri?" Tam demanded. *"Here, here, here!"*

"Yes . . ." Darwin gazed around at the others. "Oh. I thought she said *hear*. I could hear her just fine." He looked at Kurri. "That's what you meant? To surround the school?"

"Of course!" Kurri glared at him. "What did you think I meant?"

"I didn't know, because that's not a good signal," Darwin said helpfully. "Maybe next time you should say, 'Come here, come here.'"

"No one else had a problem understanding me," Kurri snapped. "And what were you doing so deep, anyway?"

"He never sticks to the strategy," Dubbo said, and waddled off. The others followed, turning their backs on Darwin one by one.

Dubbo was right, as usual. Darwin didn't mind that. But he didn't like when Dubbo—or any penguin—talked about him like he wasn't there.

And how was it his fault? Kurri's call should have been more specific. Darwin sighed and waddled after the others.

He was behind, as usual. But he was very, very clever. No matter what they thought. He just had to find a way to prove it.

4

ADDIE

Saturday morning dawned bright and sunny.

"Perfect weather for a magical quest!" Addie announced to Max the moment she bounded out of bed. "Or, you know, picking up trash."

She got dressed, washed her face, and brushed her teeth in record time. When she grabbed her backpack and left the room, Max was still stretching on his beanbag chair by the window, blinking blearily.

But Addie knew how to get Max to move quickly.

"Breakfast time!" she called, and seconds later, Max scooted out of her bedroom and down the hall.

Half an hour later, Dad dropped Addie and Max off at the entrance for the Shoalwater Islands Marine Park. Addie had the door open and her foot outside, but of course, Dad had to go over all the rules. Again.

"Stay with Liz," Dad said. "I know sometimes she lets you kids go off in smaller groups, but I want you near an adult at all times. And make sure you have your phone on you. Is it—"

"It's fully charged, and Find My Friends is turned on," Addie said quickly, raising her phone. "Come on, Dad, I know all the rules. Can I go now?"

"Just one more thing."

"*Ugh*, yes?"

Dad smiled. "Have fun."

Addie leaned over and gave him a quick kiss on the cheek, then leaped out of the car. She held the door open for Max, who was wide-awake and full of energy now.

They jogged over to the picnic tables, where Bree and Jake were already waiting. Addie saw Liz, the Eco-Guardians group leader who usually led their excursions, taking attendance. Her short brown ponytail stuck out of the blue baseball cap she wore, which matched her square-shaped glasses frames.

"Addie!" Bree exclaimed, waving. She'd tied bright

yellow ribbons in her two black braids today. They matched her yellow T-shirt, which featured a tree with the word ECO-WARRIOR spelled out in the leaves. "So, are you coming over tonight?"

"You have to, because we need you to be the tie-breaker." Jake's bright red bangs fell in his eyes as he leaned down to rub Max's ears vigorously. "Bree wants to watch some sci-fi show everybody at school keeps talking about. But there's a new documentary about sharks that looks wicked!"

"I'm definitely coming, and I vote for the documentary!" Addie said immediately, and Jake gave her a high five. Bree stuck her tongue out at them, but she didn't look upset at all.

"Fine, fine. Sharks win."

Dad had talked to Bree's mom on the phone for almost ten minutes last night. Addie had been in the next room, listening to every word. Dad was perfectly friendly, but she couldn't help thinking it sounded like he was almost interrogating Bree's mom. He even told her the story about Addie chasing the sugar glider into the woods behind Mrs. Miller's house! Addie was mortified. Although at least Dad hadn't told that story in front of Bree and Jake.

And besides, they would probably get it. Especially Jake. He was even more obsessed with animals than Addie!

"Okay, it looks like everyone's here!" Liz called, adjusting her baseball cap and smiling around at everyone. "Let's get started! Clean up first, and then we'll have some time to explore."

Addie took a trash bag and a spear along with all the other kids, and then they started making their way around the beach. There wasn't much trash to clean up today, which made Addie happy. Not that she minded doing it, but it always made her a little bit sad to see crumpled-up cans and Styrofoam cups and old napkins. There were trash cans everywhere! Didn't people appreciate how beautiful this area was? Why would anyone treat a marine park like a trash can?

Max stuck by Addie's side, his nose working overtime. He was excellent at trash cleanup. Especially when it came to finding things like all the chicken bones or wrappers that might still have half a burger inside.

Addie, Jake, and Bree kept up a steady stream of chatter as they worked. Mostly, Jake and Bree told Addie about everything that had happened at school that week.

"We had a fire drill yesterday right in the middle of our civics quiz! Lucky for Jake, he didn't study at all . . ."

"Mr. McNulty was *so mad*! By the time we got back inside, it was two minutes before the bell."

Addie was usually the most talkative person in the bunch, but she loved hearing Jake and Bree's stories, even if they made her feel like she was missing out sometimes. Jake talked at length about how crowded the animal shelter had been lately, especially with stray dogs.

"There's so many that need to be adopted. The shelter is starting to run out of room for them all!"

And Bree, as usual, rattled off all the new facts she'd learned that week about climate change. "We're losing over a trillion *tons* of ice every year. *Tons!* I read online that a trillion tons is the weight of *all living things on earth*!"

Addie nodded, her stomach tightening. She'd seen plenty of videos of glaciers melting and giant sheets of ice sliding into the sea. It made her feel hopeless and scared and really, really anxious. This was why Addie loved fairy tales—they had happy endings.

Real life didn't always feel that way.

An hour later, the group finished their cleanup and Liz led them on a walk down the beach. Addie had been to Shoalwater lots of times—it was one of the best places close to home to snorkel, after all—but she still listened, totally fascinated as Liz told them all about the amazing species of creatures that lived here. There were sea stars and urchins and mollusks and even bottlenose dolphins. But, of course, there was one marine animal that Addie loved best of all, and she found herself getting antsy, waiting for Liz to bring them up.

Finally, Liz stopped the group and pointed to a tiny island just visible out in the water. "Now, that island right there is home to a very special colony of marine life," Liz said with a smile. "Does anyone happen to know—"

Addie's hand shot up, and she blurted out the words before Liz called on her. "That's Penguin Island! There's a whole colony of little penguins. They're also called blue penguins, and they're the smallest breed of penguin. Penguin Island is actually the largest colony of little penguins in Western Australia! They eat sardines and squid and anchovies and . . . and that's all."

But that wasn't all. Addie could have gone on for another few minutes, listing all the things she knew about the cutest penguins in the world. Addie had learned from experience, though, that sometimes when this happened—and even though Liz was smiling and didn't look at all annoyed—her rambling wasn't always appreciated. Especially by adults.

"Amazing! You're a total penguin expert, Addie." Liz looked genuinely impressed, and Addie beamed at her. "If you guys want to know any other facts about blue penguins, you know who to talk to. Addie knows more than I do! And that brings me to an exciting announcement."

Addie perked up, and next to her, Max planted his

butt down on the sand and sat up straight as if Liz had just offered a treat.

"Some of you might already know this, but I'm a certified scuba group leader," Liz said. "And a few days ago, I got permission from the head of the Eco-Guardians to start a special scuba-diving group for anyone who's interested!"

A ripple of excitement went around the group, and Bree blurted out, "When can I sign up?"

Everyone giggled.

Liz waved her clipboard. "I'll have to speak to your parents first. There's a lot of papers that need to be signed. Scuba diving is amazing, but it's important to train and learn all the necessary skills. The group starts next week, and we're going to be meeting right after our Saturday morning excursions. We'll start at one o'clock, which gives you enough time to have lunch. Oh, and here's the best part—classes are going to take place right there on Penguin Island. If you've ever wanted to see penguins and swim with them underwater, this is your chance!"

For once, Addie was at a total loss for words.

Snorkeling was one thing, but she couldn't go deep under the water. But scuba diving? Addie thought of all the ocean that she had yet to explore, imagined herself flying around with the fairy penguins . . .

She *had* to do it.

"Okay, but what about sharks?" Jake asked, his tone uncharacteristically serious. "There are sharks out there, right?"

"There are, and I've seen a few on my dives! They're amazing creatures," Liz told him. "Part of the lessons that I'm going to be teaching you is how to deal with seeing different kinds of creatures like that underwater. My job is to teach you how to be as safe as possible so you have nothing to worry about. Now, who would like the forms?"

Almost everyone in the group raised their hand immediately, including Addie, Bree, and Jake. Addie read the top page eagerly with details about what the lessons would cover, and below was a paragraph about the waivers that Dad would have to sign in case of accidents and injuries.

And just like that, Addie's fairy-tale dream of swimming with the penguins was shattered.

There was no way Dad would let her sign up for this. He would take one look at these waivers and say it sounded *too risky*. Especially for someone as *impulsive* as Addie.

"What's wrong, Addie?" Bree asked. "You're going to do this, right?"

"I really want to. I'm just . . ." Addie hesitated. "I'm worried my dad will say no. He might think it's too dangerous."

"Of *course* it's dangerous!" Jake exclaimed. "Didn't you hear her? There are sharks out there!"

Bree wrinkled her nose. "Do you *want* to see sharks? Or are you *afraid* of sharks?"

"Yes," Jake replied solemnly, and Addie giggled despite herself.

"We can help you figure out a way to ask your dad so that he says yes," Bree said. "We'll come up with a strategy tonight. Forget the shark documentary. Right?" She nudged Jake, and he nodded.

"Right! Who cares about that silly documentary,

anyway. We're going to swim with real-life, actual sharks!"

Addie smiled at her friends. Almost without thinking, she reached out and put her hand on top of Max's head. It was something she always used to do when she needed comfort, and she needed it right now. Because Addie hadn't known it until this moment, but scuba diving with the penguins and exploring all the parts of the coast she hadn't been able to see yet was the most important thing in the *entire world*.

And her two best friends were going to do it! They already got to see each other every day at school. Addie couldn't bear the thought of staying on land while they scuba dived, too.

No matter what, Addie thought, *he's going to say yes.*

5
MAX

Scuba.

Yet another word for Max to learn. Addie and her friends were saying it over and over again, buzzing with excitement as they pointed to the island way out in the distance. Max watched as Addie read through the papers that Liz handed her. He didn't need any words to understand Addie's body language. She went from bouncing-on-her-toes excited to statue-still, from surprised to head hanging like she had just been punished.

"Don't worry, Addie," Bree said reassuringly as the group made their way back toward the picnic area. Max followed them, staying close to Jake. (Max really liked Jake because he always had a bag of crisps in his pocket, and he usually dropped one or two.) But Jake was too busy talking to Bree and Addie about *scuba, scuba, scuba,* along with *Dad* and *tonight*.

Max had to learn this *scuba* word fast. Whatever it was, it was really important to Addie. But he couldn't tell if she was happy or sad. She seemed to be both at the same time, which didn't make sense.

Suddenly, a new smell reached Max's nose and he stopped in his tracks. He turned around and just barely managed to stop himself from growling. Some smells were peaceful, or interesting, or delicious.

This smell was a warning.

Max gazed at the island dotted with teeny tiny penguins, and then farther down the mainland where there was nothing but sand and brush. The sky was crystal clear, but there were clouds way out on the horizon just like yesterday. He hadn't heard thunder, though.

A gentle breeze blew in from the sea, and now all Max could smell was briny smells like crabs and fish. He glared at the clouds on the horizon one last time before turning and hurrying to catch up with Addie and her friends.

Max was ashamed to admit it, even to himself, but storms made him jumpy. *Terrified* might be a better word.

It was never that way when he was a puppy . . .

*

BOOM! BANG!

"DAAAAD!"

Little Max watched curiously as Addie scrambled off her bed and scurried over to the closet. Rain pelted the window as Addie stood on her tiptoes, trying to reach the handle. The loud *BOOM* came again from outside, and Max wagged his tail. Whatever was outside, it was *loud*, and Max wanted to go play with it.

But Addie clearly did not want to play.

She finally managed to pull the door open. "C'mon, Max!" she cried, and Max grabbed Roo in his teeth before scooting in after her. Addie closed the door and sat down, hugging her knees. Max dropped the stuffed kangaroo in her lap. Addie was obviously scared, and Roo always comforted him. Maybe it would comfort her, too.

Addie clutched Roo in one hand, her other arm around Max. When Dad found them there an hour later, the storm was over, and Addie was fast asleep. Dad grinned at Max.

"What a good guardian you are, boy," he whispered.

Max's tail thump-thump-thumped against the carpet . . .

*

The thunder and the rain hadn't scared him at all back then.

Then one day, about a year ago, Max had gone out in Dad's fishing boat while Addie was busy taking tests. Max loved being out on the boat with the wind whipping his ears around and all the incredible scents the sea had to offer. Except this day, a storm came in really fast before Dad could get the boat all the way back to land.

One second, it was overcast but peaceful. The next second, sheets of rain were pouring down. Dad pulled a rain slicker on and leashed Max to a little pole near the main cabin as the waves grew stronger, tossing the boat around like a ball in a bathtub.

"Don't worry, Max! We'll be back in no time!" Dad called over the deafening sound of the rain. Max relaxed slightly. After all, Dad knew what he was doing.

But then the thunder started.

It was nothing like being huddled down in Addie's closet. Out here on the ocean, soaking wet and chilled to the bone, Max thought it sounded like the sky itself was about to come crashing down on him.

And there's no closet to hide in, he thought nervously.

The next few minutes were a nightmare. The waves tossed the little boat like one of Addie's toys in the bathtub. Lightning slashed across the cloudy sky, always followed by a *BOOM* that made Max strain against his leash.

Finally, Dad docked the boat. As soon as he unhooked Max's leash, Max bolted back to the house as fast as his legs could carry him. He burst inside and went straight to Addie's closet, and he refused to come out for the rest of the night. His entire body was trembling out of control, and he dripped rainwater all over the carpet. Dad and Addie brought him lots of treats and spoke to him in soothing voices, trying to get him to come out, but the thunder was still booming and Max couldn't move.

"It's okay, boy," Addie finally whispered, scooting inside to sit next to him. "I've got you."

And that was when Max realized that he and Addie had switched places. *She isn't scared of the storm at all.*

The next morning, Max felt back to normal. He almost forgot about the whole ordeal. But a few weeks later, there was another storm. And even though Max and Dad and Addie were all safe and sound inside the house, Max went racing into the bathroom, because there were no windows in there so the thunder couldn't get him. He paced around and around in circles, unable to stop himself.

It happened again the storm after that, and the storm after that. If the storm was in the middle of the day, Max paced around the bathroom. If it happened in the middle of the night, he would leap up on top of Addie and wake her, arms and legs flailing as she struggled to push him off, and he wouldn't stop until she opened the closet door so he could hide.

"Storm anxiety," Dad said one morning after a particularly loud storm, while scratching Max behind the ears. "Poor guy. A lot of dogs have to deal with that."

"But he never used to be afraid of storms before!" Addie said.

"That doesn't matter," Dad replied. "People get new anxieties all the time. It's the same with dogs."

Anxiety. Apparently, that was the thing making Max pace in circles and jump on Addie in the middle of the night. It was a very shameful word to Max. Because it meant he couldn't protect Addie. It meant he was the one who needed protecting.

Plus, it was all just so undignified. Max was a grown-up, well-trained dog. He taught puppies how to obey their owners' commands at the dog park. He was the guardian of his family. What sort of guardian was afraid of a little rain?

(And really, *really* loud thunder?)

"Come on, Max!"

Addie turned around and clapped her hands once, and Max broke into a trot. Behind her, he could see Dad's truck parked near the picnic area. Another breeze ruffled his fur, this one warmer than the one before. The seasons were about to change, and Max knew the next one was winter. Winter was the season with the most rain. And the most thunder.

Addie held open the door to the truck. Max noticed that all the papers Liz had given her were stuffed in Addie's pocket so Dad couldn't see. Just before he leaped into the truck, the breeze carried that warning scent again. Only this time, Max got a better sniff. And it wasn't a storm kind of warning.

It was something feral.

An animal.

Max stopped and turned around again, scanning the brush in the distance.

"Max?" Addie sounded concerned. "Are you okay?"

Max didn't see anything. But he knew something was out there, laying low in the brush. After a moment, he leaped into the little seat in the back of the truck and pressed his nose to the window. As the truck rumbled away from the beach, Max kept his eyes on the brush until it was out of sight.

6
DARWIN

The whole colony was having social time on the east side of the island. Social time was when they all gathered in smaller groups, but the smaller groups were still a big group, and their signals were flying around faster than stingrays.

Darwin always felt extra jittery during social time. He had lots of ideas and thoughts he wanted to share. Today, he had one observation in particular that he knew the others would want to hear. A very interesting—maybe even alarming—observation. But he also felt overwhelmed by all the chatter.

He waddled from little group to little group, trying to find one having a conversation he understood. First, he stopped by Tam, who was tilting her head and listening as Dubbo and Junee chatted about where some of the females would lay their eggs, because that was supposed to happen soon, but Darwin barely understood anything they were saying. Besides, he wasn't a female, and even if he was, he was too young to lay eggs, so he wasn't interested.

Next, he moved on to Kiana and Parra. Kiana flicked her wings when she saw him, and that cheered Darwin up because he knew it meant she was happy to see him.

"Hi, Darwin," she said. "How are you doing?"

"Did you see how the coast is eating the sea?" Darwin asked eagerly.

Kiana and Parra both looked at each other, then looked at Darwin. "What do you mean?" Kiana asked.

Darwin gestured toward the mainland. "The coast. The sea. The coast is eating the sea." It was the only way he could think of how to explain what he was seeing.

"The coast is eating the sea?" Parra repeated slowly.

"I'm sorry, Darwin," Kiana said. "I still don't understand."

A few more penguins approached, and Kiana and Parra began chatting with them. Darwin waddled away a little bit, moving up the hill so that he could better see the land. He needed to figure out a way to describe what he was seeing in a way the others would understand. It was low tide, which meant the coast was closer to the island and the sea was a little shallower. But every once in a while, the water was so shallow that Darwin could *see* the sand. Like the coast was gobbling up the water.

The coast is eating the sea. It made sense to Darwin!

"I never understand what he's saying."

Parra's words caught Darwin's attention. He half turned, listening to the others.

"Darwin just communicates a little bit different," Kiana was saying. "He's very clever."

"Clever?" Parra scoffed. "I heard about the hunting trip yesterday. He scared off hundreds of krill just to catch one jellyfish! How is that clever?"

"He's still learning how to hunt, that's all!" Kiana said. "Although I wish I knew what he meant about the coast eating the water. That doesn't make any sense."

Darwin stood there, thinking hard. He very much appreciated Kiana pointing out that he was clever, because it was true. But she seemed to be the only penguin in the whole community who thought so. And it was all because he didn't communicate quite the same way the other penguins did. That didn't mean his ideas were bad, though.

And he was right about the coast eating the water! He just had to figure out a way to say it that would make the others understand.

Darwin waddled his way uphill to the highest point on the island so that he could have the best viewpoint. He could see the entire community, several hundred penguins all gathered on the east side of the island. He wondered how many of them were talking about him, the odd bird who liked to be all by himself.

Solo time. That was what Darwin called it. It was like social time, only alone. He had tried to explain that to them, too. But no penguin understood solo time.

"Do you mean you want to be all alone?"

"Why would you want to be by yourself?"

"That's not how penguins are, Darwin."

That didn't make sense to Darwin. It might not be how some penguins were. But it was how Darwin was. And he was a penguin, so it logically followed that solo time was just as normal for penguins as social time.

Darwin ignored the colony and studied the mainland. Earlier, there had been a group of kids picking up trash along the beach. There had been a big fluffy animal, too—kind of like a land seal. Now the kids and the land seal were farther down the beach. As Darwin watched, the land seal stopped and turned around. At first, he was looking right at the island. Then he looked farther down the mainland toward the big area of wild, thick brambly bushes. The land seal went very still, and so did Darwin. He looked at the brush, too.

After a moment, Darwin saw it. A small red furry animal Darwin had never seen before. It was lying very, very still in the brush, like it knew it was being watched.

Darwin glanced back at the land seal, but it had turned around and was trotting away. It probably couldn't see what Darwin was seeing. He looked back and the small red animal was still there, lying in wait.

There was one call the penguins had when they were hunting in the water that Darwin never had a hard time understanding. "Sea lions!" That meant danger. That meant big animals with big teeth. That meant get back to the island. *Fast.*

Darwin always felt a little shiver of unease run through him when somebody called "Sea lions!" And right now, he had that same little shiver of unease looking at the furry red animal. Even though it was definitely not a sea lion.

Tam had taught Darwin about all the different types of creatures. Some, like humans and dogs, lived only on land. And other creatures, like krill and jellyfish, could only live in the water and not on land. Penguins and sea lions were both special because they could live on land and in water for a long time.

Because he was so clever, Darwin could identify a land creature, a water creature, and a land/water creature very quickly. He knew without a doubt that this little red creature lurking in the brush was a land creature, and that it was up to no good. He tried to reassure himself that land creatures couldn't get to the island. Except . . .

Darwin tore his eyes off the animal and looked at the water again. *The coast is eating the sea.* He ruffled his feathers impatiently. Why did that not make sense to everybody else? The coast was gobbling the water up. He could see the sand so clearly because the tide was so much lower than normal. Not so low that a human could have walked straight to the island, but it had never looked like this before.

A horrible thought occurred to him: *What if that red creature could walk to the island if the coast kept eating the sea?* And judging from the way the red animal was staring so intently at the colony, it would very, very much like to make that trip.

Darwin scurried down the hill as fast as his legs could carry him. He went straight to Tam and Dubbo, flapping his wings and interrupting their chatter about the eggs.

"There's a land creature who wants to get to the

island!" he shouted. "And if the coast keeps eating the sea, it's going to be able to walk here!"

All around him, the chitchat died out. Soon, almost the entire colony was staring at Darwin. Tam looked at him. She was not tilting her head.

"Land animals cannot walk to the island, Darwin. They can only swim. And land animals can't swim this far."

"But the coast is eating the sea!" Darwin gestured frantically at the water. Most of the penguins turned to look, although several exchanged eye rolls first.

"The low tide is lower than usual today," Kiana pointed out. "Is that what you mean, Darwin?"

"Yes . . . but also no." Darwin felt another surge of impatience. "The animal can't walk here yet, but it will be able to if the coast keeps eating—"

"The coast isn't eating anything!" Tam's response was sharp. "Darwin, you need to calm down."

"But—"

"We're done talking about this, Darwin." Tam turned back to Dubbo and started talking about the eggs again. All around him, the community went back to their chatter. A lot of the penguins were chatting about him. And laughing.

"The coast is eating the sea?"

"What does that mean?"

"Darwin doesn't know how to communicate."

Darwin lifted his head and marched back up the hill. He needed more solo time. Not because he was embarrassed. But because he wanted to figure out how to explain to the colony what he was seeing. If the coast ate the sea all up, the red land creature could walk to the island. And then . . .

Darwin didn't know what would happen then. Just that it wouldn't be good.

This was important. He just had to make the other penguins understand.

7

ADDIE

"Mom, Liz is teaching scuba diving! Can I sign up?" Bree waved the forms over her head.

"Oh, how fun! I always wanted to scuba."

Addie sat on the paisley-printed sofa in Bree's living room, Max crashed out at her feet. She watched, trying not to look envious as Mrs. Turner took the forms from her daughter. She patted the pockets of her bright red slacks with one hand.

"Let me just grab a pen," she said, hurrying into the kitchen.

Addie couldn't believe it. Bree's mom was going to sign the forms, just like that! Meanwhile, she still hadn't even figured out how to ask Dad if she could sign up. No matter how many different ways she imagined asking him, they all ended with him saying, "Maybe in a few years, honey. It just sounds a little too dangerous."

"You look like you just smelled a fart," Jake said, throwing a salt-and-vinegar crisp at her. It bounced off Addie's leg and landed in front of Max's head. His nose twitched, but he didn't open his eyes. "If you did, it was Bree, not me."

Addie smiled. "I'm just thinking about my dad," she admitted. "He's not going to let me scuba dive, I just know it."

"I don't get it," Jake said, shoving his hand into the bag of crisps. "It's not like you're asking him to just go scuba diving all by yourself. It's lessons with a teacher. Totally safe . . . unless we meet one of *them*." He gestured to the giant TV hanging on the wall of Bree's living room, where a hammerhead shark glided gracefully across the screen.

Bree flopped down into the armchair next to the sofa, putting her feet up on the coffee table. "I bet Liz can totally fight a shark and win. You should tell your dad that."

Addie helped herself to some of Jake's crisps. "He's just a worrywart," she explained. "I was ten years old before he would let me go on walks far enough that I couldn't see our house anymore. And even now, I can only do it if I bring Max with me. And he still doesn't let me stay home alone. He goes to these trivia nights with some of his friends on Thursdays, and I still have a baby-sitter!" She felt a twinge of shame as she said it, even though she knew Bree and Jake wouldn't judge her.

"Well, there's no way we're scuba diving without you," Jake said, crossing his arms. "It's not fair that you should have to miss out. And you know more about marine life than anyone I've ever met."

Bree's face brightened. "That's it! Maybe that's how we convince your dad! We make sure he knows this is an *educational experience*." She put a heavy emphasis on the last two words. "Parents love when something fun is an *educational experience*."

"That's true," Jake agreed. "It's how I convinced my science teacher to let our class watch this shark documentary during school."

Addie giggled while Bree exclaimed, "Wait, you've

already seen this? Then why can't we watch *The Edge of Pluto*?"

"Because *sharks*!" Jake cried, pointing to the screen. Addie was still laughing as she looked at the screen. Her heart banged extra hard against her chest at the sight of the hammerhead shark swimming serenely through crystal clear waters, skimming over the stunning pink coral. It looked so magical.

At her feet, Max let out a snort and opened his eyes. He stared at the crisp for a few seconds before gobbling it up, then returned to his nap. Apparently, the trash cleanup that morning had worn him out.

But Addie felt like she was exploding with excitement. She *had* to scuba. And she had until next Saturday to figure out how to get Dad to sign those forms.

Every morning that week, Addie woke up determined to talk to Dad about the scuba group. Bree and Jake texted her at least a dozen times a day, every day.

Bree

Did you ask him yet?

Jake

But every time Addie tried to work up the courage to show the forms to Dad, she totally lost her nerve. Because while Dad was out fishing every morning, Addie spent every spare second she wasn't doing her schoolwork looking up videos and information about scuba diving online to help back her argument that it was totally safe. And the more she learned, the more she knew she just had to do this. It wasn't just about seeing her friends more often, although that was definitely a bonus. It was that scuba diving truly was the most amazing thing she had ever seen. It was like flying through a real-life fairy-tale world.

But no matter what Addie came up with, no matter what angle she tried, she would have the same conversation with Dad in her head every time. He would totally understand why she wanted to do it, and then he would say the same thing.

"'Let's circle back to that when you're a little older,'" Addie told Max. He was lounging at her feet as she did her geography homework. "That's what Dad's going to say, I just know it. And you know what I think?"

Max blinked his big brown eyes. His tail thumped once against the rug.

"I think Dad only says that because he hopes by the time I'm *a little older*, I'll forget what I wanted in the first place! It's like . . ." She paused, her eyes widening. "It's like an evil spell. A curse!"

Max tilted his head, then yawned.

"Well, not this time," Addie said, tapping her pencil against her worksheet. "I am *not* going to give up on scuba diving."

Before Addie knew it, Saturday had arrived again, and it was time for another Eco-Guardians meeting. This time, they were going on a hike in the Leda Nature Reserve. Trying not to feel jealous and failing miserably, Addie watched as Bree and Jake and several of the other kids in the group turned in their forms to Liz.

Max nuzzled her hand, sensing her distress. Addie

stroked him gently behind the ears. But she didn't feel any better.

Bree and Jake hadn't given up. The three of them—four, including Max—hung at the back of the group as Liz led them through the reserve. Addie had been here several times before, and she loved it. But even as Liz told them all about the unique wildlife in the area, her mind was wandering back to how completely magical it would be to scuba dive with blue penguins.

When the group emerged from the trees and into the parking lot, Addie spotted Dad's blue truck right away. He was standing with several other parents, chatting, and Addie waved to make sure he saw her. He waved back.

"Maybe we could all go get lunch," Bree suggested. "Do you think your dad will be okay with that? Then we could all ask him together."

Addie opened her mouth to respond, then froze. Dad was walking over to Liz. Her heart started to race. All the possibilities, good and bad, raced through her mind. *He's going to pull me out of Eco-Guardians. Or maybe he heard about the scuba diving, and he wants to sign me up!*

"Why is he talking to Liz?" she whispered frantically, pointing. Bree, Jake, and Max all turned to look.

"He talked to her last week and a few weeks ago, too," Jake said.

Addie stared at him. "He did?"

"Yeah! It was the day we found that washed-up jellyfish."

"Oh." Addie remembered that day. Now, she watched Dad and Liz. They were both chatting animatedly, like old friends. "What could they be talking about?"

"I don't know, but it looks like they really like each other," said Bree. Suddenly, she gasped and clapped her hands. "Oh my gosh, Addie! This is it!"

"This is what?"

"This is the answer to the scuba-diving conundrum!" Bree gestured for Jake and Addie to move closer, and she lowered her voice to a whisper. "We need to get your dad to ask Liz on a date!"

"A *date*?" Addie yelped, just as Jake cried, "Ew!"

"Yeah!" Bree exclaimed. "Your dad doesn't have a girlfriend, right?"

"No . . ." Addie wrinkled her nose, gazing at Dad. He had taken her to his trivia night a few times. She knew all his friends: Harry, Doug, Carrie, Joe and Melissa. No girlfriends, that was for sure. "He did go on a few dates last year with a lady named Veronica, but that's it."

She didn't add that Dad had been on a date with Veronica when Addie had chased after the sugar glider in the woods behind Mrs. Miller's house. She still felt bad that Dad had ditched his date the second Mrs. Miller had called him. And she couldn't help wondering if that was why he'd never gone out with Veronica again.

"Look, they already like each other!" Bree said as Dad laughed at something Liz was saying. "You just have to convince him to ask her out!"

Jake was still making a face. "How is this going to help Addie sign up for scuba diving?"

Bree threw her hands up in exasperation. "Isn't it obvious? Addie said her dad is always worried about her. Well, if he has a girlfriend, he'll have less time to worry. Plus, if his girlfriend is an expert scuba diver, she can tell him all about how awesome it is and how it's totally not dangerous at all . . ."

"Then Liz can be the one to convince him to let me take lessons!" Addie exclaimed.

Bree beamed. "Exactly!"

"I guess maybe that could work," Jake admitted. "But how are you going to get your dad to ask her out?"

Addie was still watching Dad and Liz chat. She had to admit, Bree was right. They really did look like they liked each other.

"I'll figure out a way to bring it up," she said decisively. "This weekend."

8
MAX

Max knew Addie was up to something. She and her friends had been very excited yesterday, using a lot of new words Max had to decipher. Words like *dating* and *girlfriend*. And of course, *scuba*. Somehow, these things were all related. And whatever they meant, they were very important to Addie. But he hadn't figured out exactly why just yet.

Saturday night, Max had slept soundly, sprawled across the bottom of Addie's bed. Most days, Max enjoyed sleeping in a little late. But Sunday mornings when he heard the rattle of the tackle box as Dad moved around in the kitchen, he was happy to leap out of bed with Addie before the sun had fully risen. Sunday was the best day, because that was when the family went out on the fishing boat together.

While Addie got dressed, Max trotted over to the window. Much to his relief, the sky looked clear, and a deep sniff reassured him rain wasn't on the way.

After a quick breakfast, the three of them boarded Dad's fishing boat. Max sat at the stern, tail thumping the floor as Dad started up the motor. Soon they were whizzing out over the water, Max's ears flapping in the wind. The motor was so loud that Dad and Addie didn't talk, not until several minutes later when they were out over a nice quiet point and Dad cut the engine. Once they both had their fishing poles all hooked up and in the water, Max heard Addie clear her throat. His ears perked up.

"I saw you talking to Liz yesterday when you picked me up," Addie said. She was using that sly tone again, the one that meant she was saying one thing but thinking another thing. "She's nice, right?"

Dad was gazing out at his pole, his expression intent. "Liz? Yeah, very nice. She actually showed up to a trivia night once."

"Really?" Addie sounded extremely excited about this. "Was she on your team?"

"No, she was there with someone else." Dad reeled his line in a little bit.

Addie paused. "Like . . . a date?"

Now Dad looked at her. "I don't think so. Why?"

"No reason!" Addie's voice squeaked, and her cheeks went pink.

As the boat continued to drift, Penguin Island came into view. They were just close enough that Max could barely make out the tiny blue specks waddling down the sloping hill toward the east side.

"I swear, the low tide is just getting lower and lower," Dad said.

"She's really cool," Addie blurted out.

"Who?"

"Liz! And she knows a ton about marine life."

Dad smiled without taking his eyes off his pole. "Funny, she said pretty much the same thing about you."

"Really?"

The boat rocked gently, and the sun was beginning

to warm Max's fur. He yawned and stretched, wondering if it was too soon for a nap.

"I like her a lot," Addie said. "She just got her scuba certification."

Max's ears flicked a little. *Scuba*.

"That's— Hey, I think I've got a bite!" Dad half stood, reeling in his line. Without opening his eyes, Max took a deep sniff. He caught the scent of the fish as Dad hauled it over the side of the boat. And he caught another scent, too.

The same thing he smelled on the beach yesterday. The feral smell.

Max leaped to his feet with a low growl, startling Addie and Dad. He stalked to the front of the boat and stared hard at the mainland.

"What's wrong, Max?" Addie asked as Dad dropped his fish into a bucket. She reached out to stroke his head, but Max hunkered down and went silent. Finally, he spotted it: Halfway between the mainland and Penguin Island, a creature was moving through the water. Not swimming, but prowling.

Max took another deep sniff, and his suspicions were confirmed.

Fox.

The penguins, Max thought, picturing the tiny, defenseless creatures. *They're in danger. I have to do something—now.*

With a loud, sharp bark, Max leaped off the boat and hit the water with a mighty splash. He could hear Addie and Dad shouting his name, but he ignored their calls.

Max loved to swim, even though it took his fur hours to dry off afterward. When he was a puppy, he would swim as fast and far as he could. Now that he was older, he would take his time.

But today, he swam *fast*. He kept his gaze locked on the island and paddled his legs as hard as he could. He had to make it there before the fox.

Before long, the smell of the penguins reached Max's nose. Addie and Max had visited Penguin Island lots of times. The blue penguins were so delicate and tiny. Max pictured the fox baring its sharp teeth and put on another burst of speed.

At last, he reached the south side of the island and scrambled up the rocky shore. He broke into a run, barking loud, sharp barks.

"Run! Run! Run!"

In the distance, he could see most of the penguins waddling up the sloping hill as fast as they could. Max headed east and didn't stop until the water lapped around his paws. The tide was lower than Max had ever seen it—so low, there was a path between the island and the coast. And the fox had taken that path almost all the way to Penguin Island.

Now it was frozen, hunched down not far from Max. The breeze ruffled Max's sopping-wet fur, and he snarled.

The fox held Max's gaze for a long moment. Then it turned and slunk away, creeping through the shallow water all the way back to the beach. Max didn't move until it scurried into the brush and vanished.

Max relaxed. But only a little bit.

Sometimes, Dad, Addie, and Max would bring freshly caught fish over to Mrs. Miller's house. She raised chickens, and she had six dogs, including two

Labradors named Coco and Bean who were good friends with Max. More than once, Max had helped them chase foxes away from the chicken coop. Foxes weren't much of a danger to sheepdogs or Labradors, but they were definitely dangers to chickens—and penguins.

"They're crafty," Coco had told Max. "Really clever. And they don't give up easy."

Max knew without a doubt that this fox would try to sneak onto Penguin Island again. And next time, it probably wouldn't be alone.

Max waited until he could no longer catch the scent of the fox in the air before turning around. He could see Dad's boat speeding toward the island. The penguins were all huddled halfway up the slope, eyeing him warily. All but one penguin, who stood a little way away from the group close to the top of the cliff.

Max had never been around the penguins without Addie or Max, and he could tell his presence made them nervous. After all, his teeth were bigger than the fox's! He approached them slowly, wagging his tail to let them know he wasn't a threat.

"Don't worry, the fox is gone," he told them.

"Fox, fox, fox, fox!" The word seemed to echo around the whole colony as they repeated the new word. Max realized they had probably never seen a fox before.

"It's a predator," he told them. "Dangerous."

"Dangerous, dangerous, dangerous, dangerous!" they all shouted in unison.

Then one of the penguins waddled closer. "Are you a fox, too?"

Max tried not to feel offended. "No, I'm a dog."

"Dog, dog, dog, dog!" the penguins repeated.

The same penguin moved even closer. "How did a fox get so close to our island?"

"Do you see how low the tide is?" Max turned slightly so they could see the sand just visible in the shallow water. "There's a path. Even a human could walk here. When the tide is high, you'll have nothing to worry about. Foxes can swim, but they don't like getting wet." *Like cats*, he thought about adding, but then he realized the penguins had probably never seen a cat.

"But when the tide is low . . ." the penguin said, and Max could hear the fear in her voice.

She had every reason to be afraid, and so did all the other penguins. The fox would definitely be back. But it wouldn't have a chance at getting any of these penguins. Not if Max could help it. He was a guardian, after all.

"When the tide is low, I'll be here," Max announced. "I'll protect you."

"Protect, protect, protect, protect!"

The penguin closest to him tilted her head, her eyes shining. "What's your name?"

"Max," the gray-and-white sheepdog replied.

"I'm Tam," she told him. "Thank you for being our guardian, Max!"

"Max! Max! Max! Max!"

The penguins swarmed around Max, all thanking him profusely for his bravery, and Max sat up straight and lifted his head proudly.

Then the lone penguin who had been watching from a distance came waddling down the slope so fast, he tripped and rolled most of the way. Max let out a bark to warn the others, and they scattered as the penguin rolled to a stop right in front of Max. The penguin leaped up and gave himself a little shake. Max couldn't help but notice that most of the other penguins were looking away, almost as if they were embarrassed.

The penguin glowered up at Max. He was by far the smallest penguin of the colony, but unlike the others, he didn't seem to be happy or grateful over Max's offer.

"I've been saying all along that we're in danger because the coast is eating the sea!" the little penguin cried.

Tam tilted her head back. "Darwin, stop—"

"No! I was right, and you know it!" Darwin turned back to Max. "And we don't need any dog to help keep us safe from a fox. We can protect the colony all on our own. Your services are not required."

Max stared at Darwin in disbelief. "No? How are you going to protect yourself from foxes? Because it won't just be one. There will be more."

"More? More? More? More?" the group repeated.

Tam moved forward again. "Sorry about him. We do need your help, Max. Please."

"No, we don't!" Darwin insisted. "I can come up with a plan!"

The other penguins rushed forward, surrounding Max and pushing Darwin back until Max could no longer hear him. But he could see him, waddling back up the slope all alone. Apparently, Darwin spent a lot of time away from the others. That would make him even more vulnerable to the foxes.

As Dad and Addie climbed out of the boat and raced toward him, Max wagged his tail happily. But he kept his eyes on Darwin.

Whether he wanted Max's help or not, Max was determined to protect the colony. Even Darwin.

As he watched, the littlest penguin tripped and rolled down the slope a few feet, then hopped back up, muttering to himself. Max's ears flattened.

Especially Darwin.

9
ADDIE

Addie could not stop talking about it. Or texting about it.

Max was a *hero*.

She told Dad the story over and over again that night, even though (as he kept reminding her) he had seen it, too. The way Max swam all the way to Penguin Island. The way he'd raced over the rocks, barking ferociously. That moment when Addie had finally spotted what had him so worked up—a *fox*! An actual fox all the way out in the water, halfway to the island! It had turned tail and run all the way back to the mainland.

Not *swum*.

Run.

Because low tide was so low, any person, dog, or fox

could have easily walked from the mainland to the island. Which, as Addie reminded Dad every time she retold the story, had *never* happened before. Seeing that pathway from the island to the beach had been a shock to them both. It was the moment Addie's excitement had turned to fear. Because Max might have chased that fox away for now, but the penguins were no longer safe. Not during low tide.

The penguins had surrounded Max, chittering and flapping their wings. Addie knew she must be imagining it, but she couldn't help thinking it was their way of applauding their hero.

Of course, she texted her friends the entire tale as soon as she, Dad, and Max got home.

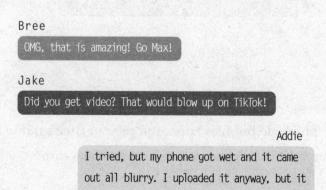

Bree
OMG, that is amazing! Go Max!

Jake
Did you get video? That would blow up on TikTok!

Addie
I tried, but my phone got wet and it came out all blurry. I uploaded it anyway, but it

doesn't have many views. I'm still really worried about the penguins. What if the fox tries again and Max isn't there? We have to do something!

Bree

Maybe the Eco-Guardians can help! You can tell everyone on Saturday and we can come up with a plan. Operation Save the Penguins!

Addie

Great idea! But I don't want to wait a whole week. We need to do something NOW.

Jake

You could call Liz, I guess?

Bree

Wait. WAIT. Doesn't Liz work at that bait shop? You know, the one right next to Star Scoops?

Addie

Yes! The Rod and Reel! I remember her talking about it.

The little bubbles appeared next to Bree's name for almost a full minute before her response came.

Bree

> I have an idea. Jake and I can be at the shop right after school—it's only two blocks away. Addie, you need to come up with a way to get there with your dad. Tell him there's a sale on fisherman stuff or whatever. And then we can put both operations into place!

Addie

> What operations?

Bree

> Operation Save the Penguins . . .

Bree

> And Operation Get Dad a Girlfriend!

Addie waited as the bubbles appeared again.

On Monday morning, Addie woke up before the alarm on her phone even started buzzing. She felt like she was practically buzzing herself. Throwing the blankets off, she crawled to the foot of her bed and gave Max a cuddle. He let out a soft growl, turning over on his side and stretching out his limbs.

"You can have a lie-in if you want," Addie said, smiling as she ruffled his fur. "But I have work to do."

Dad was already out on the water, so Addie made herself a breakfast of toast with Vegemite and an apple. She gave the entire kitchen a quick wipe-down so it would be sparkling clean when Dad got home, then poured Max's breakfast into his bowl. He trotted into the kitchen less than a minute later, tail wagging fiercely.

"Sure, *now* you're awake," Addie said, giggling. Her phone was propped up against her glass of milk so she could watch TikTok videos while she ate. Last night, she'd followed a bunch of scuba divers who took videos on their dives, and she was totally hooked. She chewed her apple slowly, mesmerized as she watched a group diving in the Bahamas, a man exploring a sunken ship off the coast of Thailand, three divers playing hide-and-seek with a sea lion in a forest of kelp, and an instructor giving a quick lesson on the sign language scuba divers use to communicate underwater.

"Max, look!" Addie said, placing her thumb on her nose and wiggling her fingers. "This means clown fish! Isn't that funny?"

Max kept his head buried in his bowl of kibble, but

his tail wagged enthusiastically. Addie wished for the hundredth time that she'd gotten a better video of Max's heroics yesterday. If only that video hadn't been so blurry! Jake was right—it would have gotten a *lot* more views.

As usual, Dad had left Addie's assignments for school written on the little whiteboard that hung on the wall in his study. That was their routine: While Dad was out fishing, Addie would read that day's chapters in her textbooks and complete all the worksheets Dad had printed and stacked on the desk. Then Dad would quiz her over lunch.

Addie's grades were pretty good, especially in biology and English. But today she put in extra effort to make sure her work was flawless. She was going to ace every question Dad threw at her.

Part one of the plan went off without a hitch. Dad made sandwiches for lunch, and Addie tried to eat, although her stomach was practically bubbling with nerves. Max lay under the table between their feet, waiting hopefully for a piece of bread as Dad quizzed Addie.

"Australia is the world's largest exporter of . . ." Dad took a bite of his sandwich and looked expectantly at Addie.

"Iron ore!" she replied promptly.

"Very good. Let's see . . . What is mined in the Kimberley region?"

"Diamonds!"

"Excellent," Dad said. "You know, geography was your mom's favorite subject."

Addie snapped to attention. Dad didn't talk about Mom too often, and she loved when he did. "Really?"

"Really." A wistful smile tugged at Dad's lips. "She used to make up the silliest songs when we'd study to try to help me remember." Dad set down his sandwich and cleared his throat. "'From the tippy top of Mount Kosciuszko to the depths of Lake Eyre fifty feet below, Australia's home to the Outback and the Great Barrier Reef . . .'"

He stopped, pretending to look offended as Addie giggled. "That doesn't even rhyme!" she managed to say.

Dad grinned. "I never said she made up *good* songs."

He stood and headed to the fridge, pulling out a pitcher of lemonade.

Addie didn't have any memories of Mom, but Dad had lots. To him, being married to Mom was probably like a fairy tale.

For a moment, Addie thought about canceling Operation Get Dad a Girlfriend. But as she watched Dad pour himself a glass, whistling the silly geography song, Addie realized something: Sometimes fairy tales had sequels. After all, every hero deserved a second chance at happiness, right?

Maybe Liz can be part two of Dad's fairy tale! she thought.

Dad settled back down in his chair. "So you and Max had a good morning?"

"Yep! I even finished early. We took an extra-long walk." Addie paused. "Um . . . you know that bait shop next to the ice cream place? The Rod and Reel?"

Dad furrowed his brow. "Yes, why?"

Addie did her best to sound as casual as possible, but her voice squeaked, anyway. "I heard they're having a massive sale today. On . . . bait."

"Okay." Dad took a sip of lemonade. "I don't need—"

"And lures! And literally everything!" Addie blurted out. "It's like a going-out-of-business sale!"

"Are they going out of business?"

Addie gulped. "No, but I mean, it's just a really big sale."

"Huh." Dad was definitely looking at her strangely. "Well, I don't see the need to drive all the way out there when I can just go to Rodney's. It's much closer."

"But you could stock up on . . ." Addie racked her brain, but it was like everything she knew about fishing had suddenly vanished from her head. "Poles? Oh, and they sell rawhide bones!" she added quickly, giving Max a little nudge with her foot.

"*Arf!*" he yelped obediently.

Good boy, Addie thought.

Dad cleared his throat. "Okay, Addie, what's really going on?"

Addie tried to look innocent, but Dad was onto her. After a few seconds, she let out a huge sigh and slumped down in her chair. "Okay, busted. Bree and Jake mentioned that they might go to Star Scoops after school and I just . . . I don't know, I'd like to hang out with them sometimes during the week, not just Saturdays."

That is so *not going to work,* she thought miserably. Underneath the table, Max let out a little whine, and Addie obediently dropped a piece of bread.

To her surprise, Dad's expression softened. "Honey, I completely understand. You don't have to try to trick me into letting you hang out with your friends. All you have to do is ask!"

"Really?" Addie sat up straighter. "So we can go?"

"Of course we can." Dad gave her a smile as he stood, picking up their plates.

Addie waited until Dad was scrubbing their dishes in the sink before ducking under the table and giving a surprised Max a hug. "We did it, boy!" she whispered. "The quest for Dad's fairy-tale sequel is on!"

Addie bounced up and down in her seat, and not just because the truck was rolling over pothole after pothole. A small part of her felt guilty for lying to Dad.

Well, not lying, exactly. After all, she *was* meeting Bree and Jake at Star Scoops. But their real mission had nothing to do with ice cream.

At half past three, they passed the school. Already, students were pouring out of the redbrick building, most gathering on the grass field west of the school and huddling in smaller groups. Addie tried to spot Bree and Jake, but with everyone wearing the same uniform, it was difficult. She glanced down at her jeans and yellow top. Bree always said she was so lucky not to have to wear a uniform. But Addie would happily wear the plaid skirt and white shirt if it meant she got to hang out with her friends every day.

Dad parked in the lot of the strip mall that included the Rod and Reel and Star Scoops. Max had stuck his head out the back window the entire ride, and now his fur was even more wild-looking than usual as Addie held open her door for him to hop out. She kept her hand on his head as they made their way toward Star Scoops. What if this didn't work? What if Liz wasn't working at the bait shop today?

They hadn't even thought to find out, although Addie wasn't sure how they would—it would've been super weird to call the shop to ask which employees were working that afternoon.

"Addie!"

Addie swiveled around and saw Bree and Jake chaining their bikes up to the rack on the other side of Star Scoops. She waved, then glanced over at Dad. Her heart skipped a beat when she saw he was gazing at the Rod and Reel.

"Since we're out here, I might as well grab a few things," he said thoughtfully.

Addie swallowed hard.

"I want to go with you!" she said as Bree and Jack reached them. Max wagged hopefully at Jake, who immediately stuck his hand in his pocket and pulled out a small handful of crisps.

Dad blinked, turning to Addie. "You want to go to the bait shop?"

"Yeah!" Addie exclaimed, giving her friends a pleading look. "I need some new, uh, bobbers."

"Oh, yeah!" Bree added. "And I want some of those

sunglasses. You know, the ones fishermen are always wearing that are, like, extra giant and reflective and kind of make you look like a robot?"

"Polarized sunglasses?" Dad looked even more confused.

"Yeah, those!" Bree said. She elbowed Jake hard, and he winced.

"And I told my mom I'd bring home some . . ." He looked at Addie with wide eyes. "Uh . . . worms?"

Addie barely managed to stop herself from groaning.

Now Dad just looked amused. "This is for one of those videos you kids make, isn't it? Are you going to try to get everyone in the bait store dancing?"

Jake's face lit up. "You've seen my TikToks?"

"Addie showed me quite a few of them," Dad said, leading the way to the Rod and Reel. "They're pretty funny!"

Addie relaxed slightly, and she, Max, and her friends followed Dad into the shop. Addie's eyes went straight to the counter, where a tall, lanky man wearing a Fremantle Football Club shirt and a navy baseball cap nodded at them. Her heart sank, and she exchanged a quiet look of despair with Bree.

Dad headed down the second aisle while Addie huddled with her friends. "What do we do now?" she whispered.

"We should've checked to see if she was working!" Bree groaned. "This was a total bust!"

"It doesn't have to be," Jake pointed out. He held up his phone. "We could make a video, like Addie's dad suggested."

"I don't think it was a suggestion," Addie pointed out.

Bree crossed her arms. "This isn't Operation TikTok! It's Operation Save the Penguins and Get Dad a Girl—"

"Hey, guys!"

Addie, Bree, and Jake all whirled around.

"Liz!" Addie yelped, her heart suddenly racing.

Max trotted over to Liz and she crouched down to give him a good ear rub. She laughed as Max's hind leg began to thump against the floor. "What are you three doing here?"

Bree and Jake both turned to look at Addie, and she felt her face start to heat up. "My dad's a fisherman!" she blurted out, just as Dad wandered around the aisle.

Liz glanced up and smiled. "Oh, hey, Tim!"

"Liz!" Dad looked genuinely pleased. "How are you?"

Bree grabbed Addie's arm and shook it hard, and Addie fought down the sudden urge to giggle.

"Good, thanks. Just got off work." Liz stood and brushed the dog hair off her jeans. "Getting some supplies?"

"Yeah, Addie told me about the big sale—"

"Scoops!" Addie cried, interrupting him. Her face went from hot to flaming when Dad and Liz stared at her. "Um, ice cream! Next door! We were going to Star Scoops. That's why we're here."

Bree kept nudging Addie's arm as she spoke. "Ask her," she whispered out of the corner of her mouth. When Addie mouthed *What?* Bree sighed and turned to Liz. "You should come with us! Since you're off work and all."

"Well . . ." Liz looked at Dad. "I do love their salted caramel. Mind if I join you?"

"Of course not," Dad said.

Bree waggled her eyebrows at Addie, and once again, she had to fight down the urge to laugh.

A few minutes later the five of them were crammed around one of the small tables on the patio of Star Scoops. Max lay at Addie's feet, his chin resting on his paws as he gazed longingly at Jake's pocket.

"So, how was your weekend?" Liz asked looking around at everyone. Was it Addie's imagination, or did her eyes linger on Dad a little?

"Actually, we had a bit of a misadventure," Dad replied, smiling down at Max. "Or rather, Max did."

"Really? What happened?"

Dad looked expectantly at Addie. "You're the storyteller in the family!"

Addie took a deep breath and then launched into the whole story. By the time she finished, her mint chocolate chip scoop was melting in her cup.

"And the problem is that Max can't be out there on the island for every single low tide," she finished.

"I mean, obviously I'm going to take him out there as much as I can, but we really need to find another solution for the fairy penguins. And Bree and Jake and I were talking about it yesterday and we think that this might be a project the Eco-Guardians could take on."

"That's a great idea," Liz said, scraping up her last bite of salted caramel. "The last thing that penguin colony needs is foxes, on top of everything else."

"What do you mean?" Jake asked, his mouth full of Neapolitan and gummy worms.

"Well, you know we've talked a lot about how climate change is having an effect on a lot of the local wildlife," Liz explained, and Bree nodded fervently. "For the penguins, the fact that the waters are getting warmer makes it harder for them to catch food, so they have to swim out farther and go a lot deeper when they hunt—which means they're more vulnerable to predators. It also means they're away from the colony a lot more, and that gives them less time to breed, which means fewer penguins. And I'm sure you've noticed that the storms get more severe every year."

At this, Max's head jerked up and he gave a little whine.

"It's okay, boy," Addie said, leaning over and scratching him behind the ears. "Max has storm anxiety," she told Liz. "He goes crazy when there's thunder."

"I'm not a fan of it myself," Liz said with a smile. "And as for the penguins, the storms cause more erosion on the island. There's that short cliff on the west side, and it's harder and harder for the penguins to get up to their nesting sites. Plus, the warmer the weather, the harder it is for them to stay comfortable."

As Bree and Jake asked more questions, Addie stared down at her melting ice cream. If Max had storm anxiety, Addie had climate change anxiety. Anytime she read about the effect it was having on the planet, it made her feel completely and totally overwhelmed and helpless.

Dad must have noticed her expression, because he cleared his throat. "Surely there's something we can do to help the penguins stay safe?" he asked, directing the question at Liz.

Liz drummed her fingers on the table. "Now that

you mention it, I remember talking to another Eco-Guardians volunteer about the penguins on Bowen Island. If I recall, the local chapter over there built nesting boxes for the penguins. They were painted with heat-reflective paint so the penguins could stay cool when the temperatures got really hot."

"That's a great idea!" Bree exclaimed.

"We could totally do that!" Jake added.

"It would be a lot of extra work," Liz said, looking at Dad. "We'd have to meet a lot more than just Saturdays to get the job done."

Addie held her breath. To her surprise, Dad said, "Count us in. This sounds like a great project."

Was it her imagination, or was his smile just a little bit more goofy than normal as he looked at Liz? Bree kicked Addie under the table, and she ducked her head to hide her grin.

"Great!" Liz said, smiling around at the group. "I'll start working on a schedule tonight and call the other members."

"Operation Save the Penguins is a go!" Bree said, and everyone laughed.

"Thanks, Dad," Addie said, but Dad was looking at Liz. Addie definitely wasn't imagining it. Dad had a really goofy look on his face.

Maybe Operation Get Dad a Girlfriend was a go, too.

10
DARWIN

The tide was high, and the penguins were preparing to go on a hunt.

"Are you coming, Darwin?" Kiana called as Darwin waddled toward the group.

"No, I don't think now is a good time to hunt!" he replied.

Kiana blinked. "Aren't you hungry?"

"I *am* hungry," Darwin said loudly, and a few of the other penguins turned to look at him. "But I'm also frustrated. We need to figure out a way to outsmart the foxes!"

"This again," Dubbo said with a sigh.

Tam shook her head. "Darwin, we've talked about this."

"You heard Max," Kiana said gently, moving closer to Darwin. "He's going to come back and help us. What else can we do?"

Darwin didn't have an answer to that. Not yet. That was why he was so frustrated. He wasn't the best swimmer, and he wasn't the best hunter, but he was clever. He had way more brains than a fox!

But all he could think to say was: "We have to figure out how to defeat them!"

"You can't fight a fox," Tam told him sternly. "If that's what you're thinking, you can just forget it."

"That is not what I'm thinking," Darwin replied. "We don't need to fight the fox. We need a plan. A strategy!"

"Because you're so good at strategies?" Ferro joked, and the other penguins tittered.

Darwin ignored this and looked at Tam. "I was right about the coast eating the ocean, wasn't I? A fox walked almost all the way here! I tried to tell you—"

"And none of us understood what you were saying!" Tam replied. She was definitely not tilting her head. "Now forget about it, Darwin."

But Darwin was not going to forget about it. He watched as the others waddled into the water, disappearing beneath the waves. Then he turned and made his way up the slope alone.

He stood at the top of the cliff, gazing out at the endless ocean. Practically every penguin in the colony had been chatting about Max nonstop. They were all counting on Max to protect them from the fox, if it decided to come back. But what if Max decided not to come back? Then what?

The penguins needed to figure out a way to protect themselves. They needed a strategy. And like Tam and Dubbo and pretty much everyone always said, Darwin was not good at strategies. But he had to try.

This was his chance to be the hero and show everyone in the colony that they underestimated him. That he was more clever than a sheepdog or a fox or any other creature.

Darwin thought about his last solo dive, when he snatched that jellyfish that had been drifting out on its own. Then he thought about the school of krill and the way they shimmered and moved almost like they were one giant sea creature—well, until Darwin caused them to scatter, ruining the penguins' hunting strategy.

Penguins were like krill, sticking together. But Darwin was more like the jellyfish, out there all by itself. Maybe that was why Darwin was so bad at strategies. He never understood what the other penguins were thinking, and they never seemed to understand him.

Darwin decided to take a solo dive. He knew Tam would probably not approve, and Kiana would tell him it wasn't safe to go out on his own. But Darwin loved being in the water, even if he didn't move like the other penguins. He had his best ideas in the water. And right now, he really needed a brilliant idea.

He hit the water with a splash, twisting happily as he plunged down to the very bottom. Darwin admired the pink coral and bright green seaweed growing between the gray rocks. He spotted a small fish skimming the top of the rocks, and his tummy rumbled. A snack would probably help him come up with an idea. But just as he surged toward it, one of the rocks opened a gaping mouth and swallowed the fish whole!

Darwin's shock only lasted a moment. Now he recognized the cuttlefish, with its long tentacles covered in suckers. Already, it was changing from gray to blue as it rose over the rocks and drifted away.

Darwin had been diving with Kiana the very first time he saw a cuttlefish. Kiana had explained that some creatures could make themselves look like something else—like a rock—to hide.

"Cuttlefish do that to catch their prey," Kiana had told Darwin. "But they also do it to hide from sharks and other predators."

Darwin stopped swimming. He stared at the spot in the rocks where the cuttlefish had been hiding.

"That's it! That's what we have to do! We have to look like rocks!"

Darwin began to turn and twist in the water. He'd done it! He had a strategy! He really was the cleverest penguin in the colony!

Granted, Darwin didn't know exactly how to look

like a rock. Blue penguins were always blue; they couldn't change colors like cuttlefish. But there had to be another way, and Darwin was going to figure it out.

He'd prove to Tam and Dubbo and Kiana and everyone that they didn't need Max at all.

11
MAX

Max and Addie checked on Penguin Island at low tide every day for the next week. To Max's relief, the tide wasn't always so low that the path was exposed. And while he didn't smell fox in the air at all, he knew there was no way the crafty creatures had given up. As soon as the tide was low enough to expose the path, the foxes would be back.

Friday afternoon, Dad took Addie and Max out to the island on his boat. As they whizzed across the water, Addie suddenly stood up and pointed.

"Look! Scuba divers!"

Scuba. Max's head jerked up, and he looked in the direction she was pointing. Another boat was in the distance, not too far from the island. A woman was standing up, just like Addie, only with her back to the water. She was wearing a shiny black suit and had a funny-looking mask over her face and something big and shiny strapped to her back. As Max, Addie, and Dad watched, the woman let herself fall backward into the water and sink. Max waited and waited, his muscles tensing. After half a minute, his instincts kicked in, and he moved forward. But when Addie put a hand on his back, he fell still.

"I bet it's amazing under there," Addie said dreamily. "Scuba diving is so cool."

Max looked at her in disbelief. *That* was scuba? Going underwater and not coming up, like a fish?

Addie suddenly turned to Dad. "There's a new scuba-diving class and Liz is the instructor and they're going to meet Saturday afternoons after Eco-Guardians and I really, really want to do it and I have the permission forms so will you sign them please, please, *please*?"

Max looked at Dad. Surely he wasn't going to let Addie do something so dangerous. The woman still hadn't come up for air! Even worse, if Addie did scuba,

115

Max couldn't go with her. He couldn't keep her safe because he couldn't go underwater for that long.

Dad was smiling. "I was wondering how long it was going to take you to ask me about that. Liz mentioned it last week."

"She did?" Addie pressed her hands together and made a face that Dad always called her *puppy dog eyes*, even though, in Max's opinion, she looked nothing like a puppy. "Did she tell you how safe it is? And how she's going to teach us how to be super responsible? And—"

"Okay, okay, I get it," Dad said, laughing. "Look, Addie, I won't lie to you. My first instinct is to tell you maybe in a few years. But . . ." He paused, gazing out to the boat where a man wearing the same kind of mask splashed into the water. "Can you just give me a few days to think about it?"

"Yes! Of course! Thank you, thank you, *thank you!*" Addie threw her arms around Dad, her eyes shining with glee.

Max could not believe what was happening. The rest of the ride to the island, he kept his eyes on the spot where the woman had disappeared beneath the waves. At last, as Dad docked the boat, he saw the woman's head pop out from the water. She took off her mask as the man emerged, too. They were both laughing. And they were both totally fine.

Even so, Max did not like the idea of Addie doing scuba.

He followed Addie and Dad onto the rocky island. The blue penguins immediately began to crowd around them—around *him*—and Max forgot all about scuba as the penguins called his name over and over again.

"Oh, my goodness, Max! They love you! And they're so cute!" Addie exclaimed, taking her phone out and holding it up. Max looked around at the penguins. He didn't see the little one, Darwin, who had been so angry before.

"Good news, little guys!" Addie told the penguins, crouching down low in front of Tam. "My friends and I are going to build you guys some nesting boxes!"

"How about we check out where the nests should go?" Dad suggested, gesturing up the slope.

"Yeah!" Addie said, and she and Dad set off together. Max lingered behind, and the penguins drew closer around him.

"Nesting boxes?" Tam asked curiously.

Max had heard Addie talk about these all week, and he was pretty sure he figured out what it meant. "She's going to build nests for you. Sturdy nests that won't be hurt by the rain and can keep you cool when it's hot."

"Will they keep us safe from the foxes?" Kiana asked nervously.

Max flicked his ears. "I don't think so. But that's why I'm here. I want to teach you some defense strategies."

"Strategy! Strategy! Strategy! Strategy!"

"Penguins are very good at strategies," Tam told him, tilting her head. "We come up with them all the time to hunt fish."

Max had never thought about penguins being hunters before. "The most important thing to remember is that during low tide, you should stay together as tightly as possible. There's safety in numbers." He paused, then started looking around. "Where did Darwin go?"

A few of the penguins muttered and looked away. Tam flapped her wings. "He's on a solo dive. He's been doing more and more of them lately. It's not safe, but he won't listen to us."

Max felt a twinge of worry that he tried to hide. "I'm sure he'll be back soon. Maybe if I have a talk with him, I can make him understand. Now, let's talk about what to do if a fox does get onto the island and I'm not here."

Max trotted closer to the coast, and the penguins waddled after him. He turned to face them and crouched down a little. "Pretend I'm a fox."

The penguins immediately clustered together tightly. Max had to admit, even though it was obvious they were afraid, he would have second thoughts about attacking so many penguins all at once. His eyes went from their beaks to their pink feet and surprisingly sharp-looking black claws.

He prowled forward a few steps, and they backed away, chattering nervously.

"The smaller penguins should be on the inside of the group," he told them. "The biggest and strongest penguins on the outside." The penguins shuffled around obediently, then waited for further instructions.

Max took another step forward. "How sharp are your claws? Show me!"

Tam and Dubbo glanced at each other. Then they both balanced on one foot and flexed the other claw. Tam tottered but kept her balance while Dubbo toppled over. He got up quickly, clearly embarrassed.

"Well, your claws look very sharp, but maybe that's not your best defense," Max admitted. "Your beaks are sharp, too. Try snapping them at me!"

The penguins all snapped their beaks. *Click-click-click-click-click!* It was a strange sound, but it wasn't exactly intimidating. Still, Max took a step back as if he were afraid.

Movement caught his eye, and he glanced over to where Dad's boat was docked. Darwin had just emerged from the ocean and was shaking the water from his feathers.

"Stop!" Max waited until the clicking had stopped,

then looked pointedly at Darwin. The other penguins turned to look at him, too. "If I were a fox, Darwin would be my target because he's alone. And what's the most important rule?"

"Safety in numbers!" the penguins chorused, and Max nodded approvingly.

Darwin waddled forward, glaring at Max. "What are you doing?"

"Teaching everyone how to defend themselves against foxes," Max told him. "And no one needs this lesson more than you."

Darwin flicked his wings. "I told you, we don't need a dog teaching us anything. For your information, I figured out a strategy."

A few penguins tittered.

"You?" Ferro said. "No offense, Darwin, but strategies aren't exactly your talent."

"He doesn't have a talent," Dubbo added.

Max couldn't help feeling sorry for Darwin. But Darwin didn't look in the least bit offended.

"I did figure out a strategy!" he said proudly. "We turn into rocks!"

The other penguins were silent. Then more giggling started up.

"Turn into rocks?"

"What does that mean?"

"Darwin never makes any sense!"

Darwin was still chattering, but whatever he was saying was drowned out by the other penguins all making jokes about him. Max watched as the littlest penguin finally turned and waddled off alone. He had to figure out a way to get Darwin to take this seriously. Because when the foxes did return, Darwin would be their number one target.

12
ADDIE

Building the nesting boxes turned out to be a much bigger project than Addie expected. The group from Bowen Island sent Liz the blueprints they used to build their boxes. The materials they needed were simple enough: Treated lumber, flathead nails, heat-reflective paint, and paintbrushes. But since the Penguin Island colony included several hundred penguins, and each box or nest could hold no more than four fully grown penguins, they had a *lot* of boxes to build. Then they would have to half bury them in the dirt to make sure they would be secure, even during thunderstorms.

All this meant that Addie spent every day with Bree and Jake after school, hammering and painting. They were also taking more frequent trips out to Penguin Island, using tiny bright orange flags to mark the spots where the rocky ground was soft enough to dig while Max looked after the penguins. Addie took lots of videos of the project in progress, and she shared them on TikTok. But each one had fewer than fifty views, and only Bree and Jake ever left comments.

Still, Addie was thrilled to be able to spend so much time with her friends. As an extra bonus, it meant Dad and Liz were getting lots of time together, too.

But by Friday evening, they'd only managed to build a dozen boxes.

"Don't worry," Liz told them as they stored the boxes in Dad's toolshed. "Tomorrow, we'll get the whole group working on it. It's the perfect Eco-Guardians project!"

"Only one problem there," Dad replied, closing the shed door. "The forecast tomorrow isn't the best. We might get rained out."

"Fingers crossed," Liz said, smiling at him.

Addie crossed her fingers. She was wishing for a lot more than sunny weather.

Saturday morning was cloudy, but not a drop of rain had fallen when Dad, Addie, and Max arrived at the beach with the truck loaded up with all the materials and tools they'd need to build the rest of the nesting boxes. Addie noticed Max staring intently at the horizon as Liz told the group about their special project.

"We're going to split everyone into three teams— one for box assembly, one to do the hammering, and one to do the painting," Liz was saying. "Addie, Bree, and Jake have been hard at work all this week, and they've already built a dozen boxes. So if you have any questions, ask them!"

The next two hours flew by. To Addie's relief, the storm held off, although the clouds were definitely getting lower and darker.

"It's okay, Max," she whispered when Max let out a little whine. "Don't worry."

Bree got to her feet and brushed the sand off her knees. "Whoa, we've built . . ." She made a show of trying to count the nesting boxes, then gave up. "A *lot* of nesting boxes!"

"Can we bring them to the island today?" a boy with curly black hair and green glasses asked. Addie was startled to realize he was looking at her, like she was in charge.

"Um." She glanced over at Dad and Liz, who were both helping the hammering team. "I think the paint takes an hour to dry, but after that, yeah!"

But five minutes later, a fat drop of rain landed on the back of Addie's neck. Another one splashed on the nesting box she'd half coated in paint, and she groaned.

"Get the nesting boxes to the truck!" Dad called, and everyone leaped to their feet. The next few minutes were chaos as they sprinted toward the truck carrying nesting boxes—most completed, but some unpainted, and others only half built. Dad pulled out a huge tarp to cover the boxes, and Max jumped into the back seat of the truck and huddled there, shaking all over.

Addie felt terrible for Max. It hadn't even started thundering yet! And it was barely raining. She was about to say goodbye to Bree and Jake when Liz called out:

"Don't forget, next week is the first scuba group meetup! If you haven't turned in your forms yet, now's your chance!"

Addie's heart started to thump.

"So?" Bree said, nudging Addie hard. "Has your dad given you a definite yes yet?"

"Not yet," Addie said with a sigh. Ever since Dad had promised to think about it, she had been too afraid to bring it up again. Because *think about it* meant *maybe*, and she was terrified if she asked again, it would turn into *no*. Several kids had gathered around Liz, handing her their forms.

"How's the operation going?" Jake asked. "Not the penguin one. The other one."

The three of them looked over at Liz as Dad joined her. "They sure seem to like each other a lot," Bree said.

"I think they do," Addie said. "I just don't know if they *like* like each other."

"You've got to get your dad to say yes to scuba diving!" Bree said impatiently. "I think you should go over there and just ask if you can turn your forms in now. Just pretend he already said yes. There's no way he'll say no."

Addie almost laughed. "Oh yes, he would. My dad is really good at saying no."

"Yeah, but not in front of Liz!" Bree insisted. "Think about it. What's he gonna say, 'Addie, I know Liz is really good at scuba diving and is a responsible teacher and also she's really pretty and I want to date her, but I'm pretty sure she'd let you drown'?"

"Or get eaten by a shark?" Jake added. "Because I think our odds of getting eaten by a shark are way better than drowning."

Addie giggled, but she had to admit they had a point. Before she could change her mind, she stood up and walked over to Dad and Liz.

"Ready to get home?" Dad asked, adjusting his baseball cap. Was it her imagination, or was he actually blushing a little bit?

"Yeah," Addie replied, then she took a deep breath. "But first . . . I have the scuba permission forms in the truck. So, um, if you want to sign them, I can give them to Liz right now."

Dad glanced at Liz, who was grinning. "I was so hoping you would sign up, Addie! I thought it was kind of funny that you hadn't yet. Scuba seems like it'd be right up your alley."

Addie nodded fervently. "It is! Ever since you told us about the group, I haven't been able to stop thinking about it. I've been watching all these videos online, ones where scuba divers take these waterproof cameras down there and, oh my gosh, it just looks so amazing! It's like a whole other world!"

"It really is!" Liz agreed. "So, you have your forms?"

Addie gave Dad a pleading look. He didn't look mad, just a little bit sad. "You really want to do this, don't you, honey?" he asked quietly.

"More than anything."

Dad looked at Liz. "And it's safe?"

A look of understanding crossed Liz's face. "Oh, of course! We spend most of the first lesson getting to know the equipment and going over all the rules and the safety procedures. We don't dive deep for a while. And we'll have multiple instructors there keeping an eye on them at all times."

Addie crossed both her fingers behind her back as Dad nodded slowly. "Okay, I give in," he said with a little smile, and Addie's heart soared.

"Thank you, thank you, *thank you!*" she cried, giving Dad a tight hug. She raced to the truck to grab the forms she had tucked into the pocket behind the passenger seat, along with a pen.

Max looked up at her, slightly startled by her excitement. He was huddled in the center of the bench seat, as far as he could get from the windows on either side.

"I'm gonna scuba dive, Max!" she exclaimed, and he let out another little whine that made her giggle. "Oh, Max, it's barely raining at all, you scaredy-cat. Be right back!"

She raced back toward Dad and Liz, the permission forms clutched tightly in her hand.

13
DARWIN

"Darwin, where are you going?"

Darwin turned around to see Kiana waddling toward him. He flicked his wings and glanced over his shoulder. "I'm going on a solo dive."

"Again?" Kiana looked nervous. "Darwin, you've been going on so many solo dives, and you never come on hunts with the rest of the colony anymore."

Darwin tilted his head. "No one wants me to come on the hunts because I mess up the strategies."

"That's not true," Kiana said, but it was true, and they both knew it. "Darwin, I can help you. You just need to learn the words that we use to communicate certain things."

"It's not just that," Darwin told her. "None of you

understand me. Like when I said the coast is eating the sea."

"I had no idea what that meant," Kiana admitted. She turned around and looked out toward the mainland. The tide wasn't low right now, but she still gave a little shudder. "But after that fox almost got to the island, I understood."

"It's going to happen again," Darwin said. "The foxes are going to be back. That's why I have to . . ."

He trailed off because he didn't want to say it again. Even though Kiana would never make fun of him.

"Figure out how we can all turn into rocks?" Kiana did not say it meanly, but Darwin knew she still had no idea what his words meant.

"Figure out how we can hide," he said, because it was the only other way he could think of to explain it.

"There's no place to hide from the foxes," Kiana said. "Even the nesting boxes won't work. I heard Tam and Dubbo talking about it. Foxes look a lot bigger than us, but they are good at slinking and squeezing into small spaces."

"Don't worry, Kiana." Darwin didn't like seeing her so frightened. "I'm going to figure out a way to protect us."

"Well, that's why we have Max!"

Darwin ignored a flash of irritation. "Whenever he decides to come to the island, sure. But I don't think he's going to be here for every low tide. But it's okay, Kiana. Trust me!"

With that, he turned and waddled off the edge of the cliff, hitting the water with a mighty splash.

As usual, Darwin dove all the way to the very bottom until the water was dark. After seeing the cuttlefish that had disguised itself as a rock, Darwin had started to notice that lots of creatures in the sea could hide themselves just like that. There were flatfish that half buried themselves in the sand, their spotty brown gills allowing them to blend in almost perfectly. There were big, beautiful crabs with shells the exact color of the coral, and they were only noticeable when they began to crawl.

Today, Darwin explored a big patch of bright green seaweed. He swam over it slowly, skimming the top with his feet and looking for anything that might be disguising itself. To his delight, he spotted a bright green sea dragon as it gave a little shimmy and rose up from the seaweed.

Darwin twisted and turned in the water as he thought hard. So many of the creatures that could hide themselves did it with their color. But he and the other penguins could not change the fact that their feathers were blue. Darwin had always liked their blue feathers. But blue didn't blend in with any of the colors on the island. He couldn't make himself the golden brown of the sand, or the gray and brown of the rocks, or the bright green of the grass. There had to be another way . . .

Darwin stopped his twisting and turning and stared at the patch of seaweed.

"Darwin, you're a genius!" He began to tug as many strands of seaweed out of the bottom of the sea as he could.

He soared back up to the island and waddled over the rocks, dragging the seaweed behind him. Most of the colony was huddled together on the east side of the island, but he could see a few moving up and down the slope and inspecting the handful of nesting boxes that had been installed. Darwin found a nice thick patch of grass and compared the color to the seaweed. They weren't the exact same shade of green, but they were pretty close. He wrapped himself up as best he could in the seaweed, first his webbed feet and then his body and his wings and as much of his head as he could, leaving a little slit for his eyes. Then he nestled himself into the grass and waited.

Ferro and Kiana came waddling down the slope, chittering away. Darwin held his breath.

"The nesting boxes are really cozy, although I think I'd like to bring a little more grass into mine . . . Darwin?"

Kiana came to a halt not far from where Darwin was trying to be grass. He closed his eyes tight, but it was too late. Kiana moved forward a little closer and pulled off some of the seaweed. Darwin groaned.

"Darwin, what are you doing?" Kiana's face softened. "Are you trying to be grass?"

"Yes," Darwin admitted. "I guess it didn't work."

Ferro started to giggle. "You were trying to be grass? What does that mean?"

"Darwin is trying to figure out a way to keep us safe from the foxes," Kiana told Ferro. And even though she didn't say it in a mean way, Ferro started to giggle even harder.

Darwin sighed, shaking off the seaweed. He appreciated Kiana's support, but he could tell she didn't really understand. Still, he was determined to figure it out.

The next morning, Darwin woke up extra early. He was picturing the flatfish half buried in the sand. It had two eyes right next to each other on the top of its head, and they were the only way Darwin could see it. Of course, the flatfish was the same color as the sand, and Darwin was not. But maybe if he buried himself a little bit deeper . . .

As the sun rose over the ocean, Darwin got to work. He found the softest patch of sand he could and began to dig with his wings and claws. Then he lay down flat on his back and covered himself up with as much of the sand as he could. When he was done, the only thing sticking out of the sand was his beak and the tips of his webbed feet. He even covered his eyes so that no one could spot him the way he'd spotted the flatfish.

Darwin felt thrilled with himself as he listened to the sounds of the rest of the colony waking up. There were a few distant splashes as several of the penguins dove straight into the water for some breakfast, while others came waddling down the slope in his direction. They were all going to pass right by him, and the moment the last penguin had waddled by, Darwin would leap up and show them all that he had been sand the whole time and they hadn't seen him! Then he would teach all of them how to bury themselves in the sand like a flatfish and the foxes would never find them. He would be the hero of the colony.

"It's a little cooler this morning," he heard Dubbo saying, and Darwin tried not to wiggle with excitement. "I think the seasons are changing, and . . . YEOW!"

Dubbo's fat webbed foot landed right on Darwin's

face! They both yelped, and Darwin leaped out of the sand. He rubbed his sore beak while Dubbo hopped on one foot. The penguins all stopped and stared at Darwin.

Dubbo glared at him. "Darwin, what in the world were you doing?"

Before Darwin could respond, Ferro appeared. "Let me guess," he said teasingly. "You were being sand?"

The other penguins started to titter, and Darwin flipped his wings in frustration. "It was working! None of you saw me! The foxes wouldn't have seen me either!"

Tam approached, and she was not tilting her head. "Darwin, I thought you were going to drop this! You hurt Dubbo's foot!"

Darwin stamped his own foot. "He hurt my beak!"

Dubbo looked extra cross. "Your beak had no business sticking out of the sand!"

"I . . ." Darwin started to respond but then decided not to. The other penguins were still giggling, and Dubbo and Tam looked angry. Until he was successful at figuring out how blue penguins could turn into something else that could hide from foxes, there was no point in trying to explain it to them.

That afternoon, Darwin went on another solo dive. He managed to catch a few krill, but he didn't spot any new creatures hiding. Then he saw a dark shape moving fast across the bottom of the sand. At first, he thought it was a shark. Then he realized it was a shadow, and he looked up. There was a boat speeding toward the island. And while lots of boats visited the island, Darwin had a sinking suspicion he knew who was on this boat, because they'd been visiting more and more lately.

Sure enough, when he scrambled back onto the rocks, he saw Max trotting out to greet the colony while the girl and the man who were usually with him carried more nesting boxes up the slope. Darwin started to shake the water off his feathers, then caught sight of his webbed feet covered in sand. The water made the sand cling to him. Maybe that was the answer!

As quietly as possible, Darwin rolled around in the

sand until his blue feathers were dark brown. He could hear the snapping of the penguins' beaks as Max led them through their drills.

"Remember the first rule!" Max was saying, and the penguins responded immediately.

"Stick together! Safety in numbers!" they shouted.

Darwin rolled his eyes. He looked around and spotted a sandy mound with weeds sprouting out of it, and he waddled over as fast as he could. He crawled into the weeds and doused himself with even more sand. Just as he finished, he heard Max say, "Where's Darwin? He shouldn't be off on his own!"

"He went on a solo dive again," Tam responded, sounding annoyed. "I've had many talks with him, but he just won't listen. He should be back by now."

"I'll take a look around," Max said. "Keep practicing!"

The penguins obediently went back to snapping their beaks. Darwin squeezed his eyes closed and waited. He could hear the sheepdog sniffing, the sound getting closer and closer, and he realized the sand probably did not cover up the smell of penguin as well as it covered up the blue of his feathers.

Sure enough, a few minutes later, Max's cold nose was poking right at Darwin.

"Okay, okay," he grumbled, shaking himself off and stepping out of the weeds. Max was staring at him, looking as bewildered as the other penguins had.

"Were you trying to hide?"

"Yes," Darwin admitted. "But just because you found me doesn't mean a fox would have."

Max sat back on his haunches. "Foxes use their noses just like dogs. The way you smell is even more important than the way you look. A fox would've been able to find you, Darwin. You're . . . *impulsive*." *Just like Addie*, he found himself thinking. "You need to think before you act, and stay with the—"

A loud *crack-crack-crack BOOM* cut Max off. Darwin spun around quickly.

"Look, Dad, fireworks!" the girl cried, pointing toward the harbor in the distance. Darwin relaxed slightly as he saw the familiar explosion of colorful lights over the water. The humans did this sometimes when they had festivals and parties on the harbor. Darwin didn't much like the noise, but the lights were pretty, especially when they happened at night and lit everything up like daytime. It wasn't dark yet, but the sun was beginning to set, and the fireworks were beautiful against the purple sky.

When Darwin turned around, he was surprised to see Max was now huddled right in the pile of weeds Darwin had been trying to hide in! Max's tail was tucked between his legs, and he was shaking all over.

Darwin stared at him. "Are you afraid of fireworks?"

Max straightened up a little, although Darwin could see he was still shaking. "Fireworks? It sounded like thunder! Are you sure it wasn't thunder?"

Darwin gestured with his wing out toward the harbor in the distance, just as there was another *crack-crack BOOM!* Max recoiled but relaxed slightly when he saw the sparkling lights exploding over the water. He emerged from the weeds, his head hanging low as he started to pace around in circles.

"Not a storm, not a storm," he said over and over again.

Darwin stared at him in complete disbelief. "Storms scare you," he said. It wasn't a question.

Max stopped pacing and turned to look at him. He raised his head defiantly, then dropped it with a sigh.

"Don't tell anyone," he said, and Darwin nodded. "They didn't used to scare me but . . . Well, now they do. I was out on the boat when a storm hit once, and it was really frightening. Now every time I hear thunder . . ."

He didn't go on, but Darwin understood. He pictured the way the waves tossed during a big storm. He could imagine how frightening it might be to be out on a boat in the middle of that, especially if you couldn't dive deep beneath the waves and stay there until the storm stopped.

He was more than a little pleased to hear that Max wasn't so brave after all.

"Penguins aren't afraid of thunderstorms," he told Max. "Even though the winds can blow so strong, they could easily carry one of us away!"

Max glanced up at him. "You're right, they could. What do you do during a storm?"

"We huddle together," Darwin replied immediately. "We stay really close because when we're all together, we are stronger. The wind can't knock us all down or carry all of us away."

Now Max looked amused. "That sounds like the advice I've been giving you about the foxes—the advice that you seem determined not to take."

That surprised Darwin, because it was true. He would never have solo time during a storm.

"Foxes aren't the same as a storm," he replied at last.

"Oh, really?" Max cocked his head. "If a penguin leaves the huddle when the winds are blowing hard, the winds might get him, right? How is the fox any different?"

Darwin didn't respond. He hated to admit it, but Max was right.

"I know you like to go off on your own," Max said. "But right now, it's just not safe."

"Everyone thinks we're safe thanks to you,"

Darwin told him. "But you can't always be here when the foxes come. That's why I'm trying to find another way to protect the colony."

"The best thing you can do is come join us when I teach lessons," Max said.

Darwin flipped his wings. "I think you're the one who needs lessons. Lessons on how to not be afraid during a storm."

Max looked thoughtful. Then, to Darwin's surprise, he said, "Could you teach me how to not be afraid of a storm?"

Darwin raised his head, unable to believe his ears. This great big dog wanted lessons from him? As clever as Darwin was, he was used to no one appreciating it. "Yes, of course I could!"

"And in return, will you let me teach you how to protect yourself from the foxes?"

Darwin glanced over to where the colony was still huddled together, snapping their beaks and trying to sound scary. "I just don't know if your way is going to work," he told Max.

Max looked at the penguins, too. "I know," he said

quietly. "But maybe if we put our heads together, we can figure out a better solution."

Now Darwin was truly shocked. "You mean . . . you want to plan a strategy . . . with me?"

"Yes, that's exactly what I mean."

Darwin wiggled happily. "It's a deal!" he said, and Max's tail thumped against the ground.

14

ADDIE

Addie had been flying high all week. There was now a countdown going on in her head. *Six days until scuba. Five days until scuba. Four days until scuba.*

But her good mood was shattered when she, Dad, and Max visited Penguin Island on Wednesday.

"That's the lowest tide yet," Dad said, pointing. Addie couldn't believe her eyes. The pathway was now clearly visible, with barely enough water to cover her feet.

"I could literally walk all the way back to the mainland!" she cried, staring at the brush as if a fox might dart out at any moment and speed toward them. But of course, no fox would do that while humans were on the island. And definitely not with Max there.

"There's got to be something else we can do," she said desperately. "Max can't be out here for every low tide. And if it's just going to get lower and lower like this . . ."

Addie stopped talking, because it was happening again. That feeling of helplessness she got when she thought about how the weather and the world were changing in more and more extreme ways, and it seemed like there was nothing she could do to stop it. Dad placed a hand on her shoulder and squeezed.

"We'll figure it out," he said reassuringly. "The first step is these nesting boxes, right?"

Addie took a deep breath. "Right."

Addie and Dad got to work, digging holes and half burying the six nesting boxes they'd brought. Addie thought the design of the nesting boxes was very clever, even if it made them a little more difficult to build. There was a tunnel that led to the actual inside of the box. That way, the penguins would be protected from the wind. And the opening where the tunnel curved around into the actual nest was just big enough for a blue penguin. So long as the penguins were inside their boxes, they would be safe.

The penguins all started to chitter, and Addie glanced down the slope to see them surrounding Max and clicking their beaks. Smiling, Addie stopped shoveling dirt and took a video on her phone. "They *love* Max," she told Dad, who nodded in agreement.

"He's their hero!"

Addie sent the video of Max and the penguins to Bree and Jake. Jake's response came less than a minute later.

Jake

You NEED to put this on TikTok!

When Addie reached the top of the slope, Dad waved at her, then put his finger to his lips. He pointed, and Addie crept over to where he was standing. For a horrible moment, she thought a fox was lurking in the weeds—but then she realized Dad was smiling.

At first, all she saw was a group of rocks. Then she spotted it. The smallest penguin in the whole colony was squeezed between two rocks, standing still as a statue.

Addie couldn't help but giggle. "What's he doing?"

Dad looked amused, too. "I don't know. That's really weird behavior for a penguin. What an odd little guy."

"I hope he's okay." Addie moved forward cautiously, holding up her phone to take a video. "Hey, there! Are you pretending to be a rock?"

The penguin didn't move. Not until Addie was right in front of him. Then he gave his wings a little shake and took off, waddling to the edge of the cliff. Addie hurried after him, taking a video as he dove off the edge and disappeared into the water.

Still laughing, she started to text the video to Bree and Jake. Then she stopped and opened TikTok instead.

This one should do better than the others, she thought, and hit the + sign at the bottom of the screen.

Addie's video didn't just do better. It did a *lot* better.

By Thursday afternoon, Addie's video had over *two*

thousand views. There were tons of comments, too, from Bree and Jake and a lot of other kids in Eco-Guardians but also from other people all over the world! Addie had to admit, Jake had been right. Everyone loved the littlest penguin.

"Addie! Mrs. Miller is here!"

Addie and Max leaped off her bed at the same time and hurried down the hall. Dad was hanging up Mrs. Miller's coat, and her Labs Coco and Bean rushed forward to do their usual sniffy dance with Max.

"Hey, guys!" Addie said, squatting down to give both of them hugs. "Hi, Mrs. Miller!"

She tried to sound enthusiastic. Addie liked Mrs. Miller a lot. Mrs. Miller loved watching murder mystery shows, and she always let Addie have whatever snacks she wanted. But Addie had tried and failed once again to convince Dad to let her stay home alone while he went to his trivia night. Having Mrs. Miller here just made her feel like a baby.

"Wish me luck!" Dad said cheerfully as he pulled on his jacket. "Tonight's topic is architecture. Not exactly my area of expertise, but Joyce knows her stuff, so I think we have a chance."

"Good luck!" Addie gave him a quick hug, then added in the most casual tone possible, "Is Liz going to be there?"

Dad blinked, then narrowed his eyes. "You've been talking an awful lot about Liz lately."

Addie put on her most innocent face. "You said she'd been at your trivia night before! I was just wondering . . ."

"She might be there," Dad said evasively, pulling on his baseball cap. "And if she is, I'll tell her you say hi."

After dinner, Addie and Mrs. Miller settled in front of the TV to watch another episode of Mrs. Miller's newest favorite series, which was about a retired chef who moved from London to a small town on the coast and found herself solving lots of local murders. Addie gave Max, Coco, and Bean each a rawhide bone, which they took out onto the porch.

In this episode, someone had poisoned the batch of muffins the chef made for a community potluck, and she had to find the real culprit to clear her name. It was really good, but Addie couldn't stop checking her video on TikTok. The views were still racking up, and so were the comments.

This is the cutest thing I've ever seen!

There are PENGUINS near your HOUSE? AWESOME!!

PLEEEEEEEEASE share more penguin videos!

"What is it that's so interesting on that phone of yours?" Mrs. Miller asked teasingly.

"I took this video on Penguin Island yesterday, and a lot of people are watching it!" Addie shuffled closer to show her the video of the littlest penguin squeezed between two rocks.

Mrs. Miller was delighted. "What a silly little thing! What on earth was he doing?"

"I don't know, but he's a funny one," Addie replied. "He's kind of a loner. I've noticed he's never with the other penguins."

Mrs. Miller's smile faded. "That's a little troubling, given the fox issue."

Addie's stomach knotted up. "I know. I've been taking Max out during low tide as much as I can. I can't believe the foxes can just walk to the island now. It never used to be that way."

"Lots of things are changing," Mrs. Miller said with a sigh. "Every winter gets hotter, every year seems to bring worse storms than the last . . ."

Addie's palms went clammy. "And we can't do *anything*. I hate it."

Mrs. Miller pushed her wire-rimmed glasses up on her nose. "Well, that's just not true."

"I know we can do *some* things," Addie admitted. "We can do beach cleanups, and recycle, and build nesting boxes for the penguins, but those things are so *small*, and the changes are so *big*."

Mrs. Miller reached out and patted Addie's hand. "But that's just it," she said with a smile. "Lots of people doing small things to help can add up to *big*. Right?"

Addie returned the smile, even though her stomach was still tight. "Right."

"Take the whole issue at the animal shelter," Mrs. Miller said. "They're nearly full to capacity with stray dogs."

"Oh, yeah!" Addie said. "My friend Jake volunteers there. He told me about that."

"I'm thinking about adopting another dog, maybe two," Mrs. Miller told her. "Coco and Bean could always use the help guarding the chicken coop. Now, if I could rescue every stray dog in Australia, I would! But that's too *big*. Doesn't mean I can't do anything, though! Every adoption helps."

"You're right," Addie agreed. "Every little bit helps."

They went back to watching the mystery show, but Addie was still thinking about their conversation. She understood what Mrs. Miller was saying.

But she couldn't help thinking that Penguin Island needed *big* help. And she didn't know if all the small things she and Max and her friends were doing would be enough.

15
MAX

Max gnawed on the last nub of his rawhide bone. As usual, Bean had finished his first, and now he was eyeing Coco's closely as she took her time with it. But Max kept his gaze on Penguin Island down the coast. The tide was high so he wasn't worried about foxes at the moment, but he couldn't stop thinking about Darwin. Would the little penguin keep his promise to stick to the pack?

Then there had been the shameful display during the fireworks. Max chided himself every time he remembered how he had tucked his tail between his legs like a scolded puppy when the noise had begun. He was relieved only Darwin had witnessed this, and not the entire colony. They certainly wouldn't see him as a guardian then!

"Are you going to finish that?" Bean asked, and Max realized he'd dropped his rawhide nub. He nudged it toward Bean with his paw.

"What's on your mind, Max?" Coco asked. Her bone was only half finished, carefully balanced between her two front paws.

"Foxes," Max replied, and Bean's head shot up.

"Where?!"

"Not at the moment." Max was amused. "Do you see that island out there?" When Coco and Bean both turned to look, Max continued, "It's the home of a penguin colony. And lately, the low tide has been getting so low that it's actually possible to walk all the way to the island from the beach. A few weeks ago, I stopped a fox halfway to the island. Addie and I have been going as often as we can during low tide, and I've been trying to teach the penguins how to defend themselves, but . . ."

"We've been to Penguin Island a few times," Coco told him. "The penguins are very friendly, but they're not exactly fierce. No more so than a chicken."

"A chicken can definitely do a little bit of damage

with its beak and its claws if it wants to," Bean added. "But it's no match for a fox."

"I know." Max lowered his head glumly onto his paws. "And there's one penguin in particular, the smallest one in the whole colony, who insists on going off on his own all the time. I'm worried about him." He paused. "I'm worried about all of them."

"Was the fox nomadic?" Bean asked.

Max lifted his head. "What do you mean?"

"It means he doesn't have a pack," Bean replied. "Dogs stick together, but foxes don't always stick with other foxes."

"Sometimes they wander around alone and don't stay in one place for long," Coco added. "Maybe that fox has already moved on."

"I've seen it a few times in the brush down the beach," Max said. "Although I haven't spotted it this week."

"Maybe we should take a walk and check out the brush?" Coco got to her feet, discarding the rest of her bone. Bean seized his opportunity, lunging forward and gobbling it down quickly. Then the three of them stretched and padded off the porch steps and headed down the beach.

Max could just make out the tiny shapes of the penguins on the island. Since the tide was high, there was plenty of water between the beach and the penguins.

"It's hard to imagine walking all the way out there," Coco said.

Max agreed. "I've lived here my whole life and it's the first time I've ever seen the tide that low."

"Things are changing," Bean said. "Do you remember that one storm last summer? It was the worst one I can remember! I was worried about the chickens the whole time with those winds."

Max didn't respond. He didn't want to think about how much worse the storms were going to get this year.

The three dogs reached the brush, and instantly all their hackles were raised. The smell of fox was strong, and Max could sense the presence of the animals.

None of them spoke now. They moved as quietly as they could through the brush, sniffing intently. A few minutes later, Coco let out a soft growl, and Bean and

Max hurried over to join her. She was staring at a little hole in the ground, nearly covered by brush.

"That's a fox den," she told Max gravely. "I don't think we're dealing with a nomadic fox here. There's several of them, and they've made this their home for now."

Max stared at the hole, and he knew Coco was right. The scent of fox was overwhelming, and he knew there was more than one. They were just biding their time, waiting for a low tide when Max wasn't around to stop them. He shuddered to think about what they might be planning to do next.

The next morning, Max slept in while Addie did her schoolwork. He woke with a start when she came banging into her room with a huge smile on her face.

"Good morning, lazybones!" she said, giving him a quick snuggle as he yawned and stretched. "Dad's actually letting me go to the movies with Bree and Jake tonight . . . by ourselves!" She already had her phone out, her thumbs flying over the screen. "I think he had a lot of fun at trivia last night. He said Liz was there, and they talked a little bit. Then he asked me why I was being so annoying with all my questions, which, rude. Still, I think that's why he's in such a good mood!"

Max was too tired to decipher any of this. But he was happy that Addie was so happy.

After lunch and a long walk on the beach, during which Max was pleased to see the tide was high enough to protect the penguins, they returned to the house. Addie spent the afternoon watching videos on her laptop of people doing scuba, sinking way down deep into the water and swimming around with fish and crabs and even sharks. Max still couldn't believe that Dad was going to allow Addie to do this. And as he watched her excitedly get ready to go out with her friends that evening, he felt a pang of sadness. He had always been Addie's best friend. Now she was getting older and had other friends and interests like scuba, and Max couldn't help feeling like he didn't have a purpose anymore.

He had always been Addie's guardian. Maybe she didn't need one now.

So where did that leave Max?

He spent most of the evening curled up on the sofa with Dad, watching a movie that thankfully did not have bangs and booms. Max was starting to doze off when a loud knock at the door caused him to leap off the couch, barking ferociously.

"It's okay, Max, it's okay," Dad said, getting up and hurrying to the door. He pulled it open, and a man wearing a cap and carrying a small box took a step back at the sight of Max. "He's harmless," Dad said, and the man offered Max a smile.

Max relaxed slightly and stopped growling.

"First time I've delivered way out here," he said, holding out the small package. "Beautiful view you've got!"

"Thanks!" Dad smiled as he took the package. "I don't have a lot of things delivered, but this is a gift for my daughter. I couldn't find it at any of the shops around here, so I ordered it online."

"Hope she likes it!"

"Oh, I'm sure she will."

Then the man waved and headed back toward his truck. Dad went back inside, but Max stayed on the porch. He watched as the man started up the truck and rumbled off down the road.

Something was wrong.

Not the man—he hadn't been a threat at all. Max took a deep sniff, but at first all he could smell was the gas fumes of the truck. But as the truck got farther away, Max detected it.

Foxes.

Max didn't hesitate. He leaped off the porch and charged down the beach as fast as he could, barking at the top of his lungs. He was distantly aware of Dad calling after him, but he didn't look back. The tide was low, and he saw with a surge of alarm that the path was exposed. And right in the center, creeping toward the island, were not one, not two, but *five* foxes.

Coco had been right. They had made themselves a home in the brush, and they were just biding their time. Max's barks grew more frantic and deep as he charged down the path after the foxes, seawater splashing in his wake. All five of them froze and turned to look at him warily. Max slowed to a halt and planted his paws in the wet sand, baring his teeth and growling. He didn't actually want to fight any of the foxes. But he would do it if he had to.

He heard footsteps behind him and knew Dad was coming. The foxes were perfectly still for almost an entire minute. Then, one by one, they slunk away, taking the long way around Max and then speeding back toward the beach. Max turned and watched until they disappeared into the brush.

Dad splashed through the water and reached him, letting out a low whistle. "Good boy, Max," he whispered. But Max could hear the worry in his voice. They both turned and looked at the island, where the silhouettes of dozens of little penguins were visible against the sunset.

That had been a close call. And it had only been luck that Max had come outside, thanks to the delivery guy. He let out a little whine and nudged Dad's hand. Dad reached down to stroke his head.

"I know, boy, I know," Dad said quietly. "We need to do something, or those little guys won't be here much longer."

16
ADDIE

"You're going to get the most amazing videos ever!" Jake examined Addie's new phone case, which was blue and green and made her phone twice as thick.

"Can you really dive with it?" Bree asked, her eyes wide. "Like, *deep*?"

Beaming, Addie took her phone back from Jake. "It's a special case, just like the ones all the divers I follow on TikTok use," she explained. "My dad got it for me as a surprise so I can get a video of the penguins swimming when we scuba dive."

"I can't believe your dad went from not wanting you to scuba dive at all to getting you a waterproof phone case," Bree said. The three of them had just finished their packed lunches and were packing away their reusable containers. "I wonder what— Oh! Do you think it was Liz's idea?"

Addie looked over to where Liz and a few other instructors were arranging all their scuba equipment on the rocks. Her heart skipped a beat at the sight of the tanks and masks. "Maybe? I don't know! He gets all weird when I try to ask him about her."

"I mean, she went to that trivia night again," Bree said. "I think they like each other. I think Operation Get Dad a Girlfriend is going just as well as Operation Save the Penguins!"

That morning, the Eco-Guardians had finished installing the last of the nesting boxes. Addie took over a dozen videos of all the penguins inspecting their new homes and making themselves comfortable while Max snuffled around, personally approving each and every nest. She was proud of everything they'd done— although she couldn't stop thinking about how the nesting boxes might not be enough for Operation Save the Penguins.

Dad had told her that morning about Max chasing off five foxes. Addie shuddered to think what would've happened if Max hadn't been there. If five foxes had made it to the island . . . She looked around at all the blue penguins chittering away as they waddled from box to box. It broke her heart to think about the damage the foxes might have done. And she couldn't help but worry that next time, the penguins might not be so lucky.

Operation Save the Penguins needed *big* help.

"Okay, are you guys ready to get started?" Liz called, and Addie shoved all her worries out of her mind. Finally, it was time for her first scuba-diving lesson!

Liz and the other instructors spent almost forty-five minutes teaching Addie, Bree, Jake, and five other kids from Eco-Guardians how to put on all the equipment. And there was a lot of equipment: A wet suit, a mask, fins for her feet, the big heavy scuba cylinder that went on her back, a BCD (which Addie learned stood for a buoyancy control device), a low-pressure inflator hose, and a regulator with a submersible pressure gauge. Addie listened as closely as she could, wishing she could take notes as Liz explained how to open the valve to check on the pressure.

"It's okay if you're not getting all this right now," Liz told them reassuringly. "All your instructors will be underwater with you, guiding you through everything. We won't let anything happen to you! Are you guys ready to get in the water?"

Addie cheered along with the others, her stomach flip-flopping just like her feet as she plodded across the sand.

"Look, Max! I'm a penguin!" she called, waddling a bit in her flippers. Max trotted over as she drew closer to the water, and he let out a little whimper. Addie reached out and let him sniff her fingers. "Don't worry, boy. This is totally safe, I promise!"

She splashed into the water with the others, and they waded out until they were waist-deep.

"Now, let's go over the hand signals one more time," Liz said. "What does this mean?"

She made a thumbs-down gesture, and Addie called out with the others: "Go deeper!"

"Good! How about this?" Liz gave them a thumbs-up.

"Go up!"

"Great!" Liz beamed. "Now . . . Addie, what's the signal if you notice your air is getting low?"

Addie instantly made a fist over her chest.

"Perfect! Bree, what if you needed to share air with Addie? What's the signal?"

Bree turned to Addie and placed her palm on her mouth, then extended it out.

"Excellent!" Liz said.

"And this means *clown fish*!" Addie added, sticking her thumb on her nose and wiggling her fingers. "I learned that on TikTok."

"What about this signal?" Jake asked, and everyone looked as he pressed his palms together over his head like a shark fin.

Liz laughed along with the others. "Sorry to disappoint you, but I doubt we'll be seeing any sharks today," she said. "Although, Jake, maybe you could show everyone the signal for danger?"

Jake made an X across his chest with clenched fists, then pointed.

"Great job!" Liz smiled. "Are you guys ready?"

"Yes!" Addie exclaimed with the others. For the

first time, she actually felt a little bit nervous. After Liz had double-checked their equipment, she gestured for them to walk out farther.

"There's a ridge just behind me with a steep drop," she told them, moving backward. "When you step off, you'll descend about thirty feet, which is deep enough for our first lesson. Remember to always stay within sight of me or one of the other instructors. Okay sign if you're ready!"

Addie gave an enthusiastic okay sign, as did the others. Liz returned the signal, snapped her mask on, took a step back, and disappeared beneath the water. Addie checked her phone to make sure the video app was recording. She followed Bree and Jake, watching as they stepped over the ridge and sank into the water. It felt incredibly strange to be this far out in the water wearing heavy equipment and carrying her phone. Addie glanced back and saw Max watching her with an expression so worried it tugged at her heart a little. She waved at him, and then she stepped over the ridge and allowed herself to sink down, down, down.

A stream of bubbles trailed from her mask, and

Addie felt like all her worries were drifting away with them. The heavy equipment didn't feel heavy at all anymore; in fact, Addie felt lighter than air. She checked to make sure her phone was still filming, then took a little video of Bree and Jake waving wildly. She couldn't see their facial expressions because of the masks, but she was positive they were beaming. And she was, too.

She felt like she'd dropped into a fantasy world. All around her, the water was crystal clear, with the surface shimmering bright white over her head. In the distance, she could see where the water grew deeper as the coast dropped away, and it was a brilliant blue. Addie drew deep, slow breaths as she practiced kicking her flippers and swimming forward. *This must be what flying feels like!* She let out a giggle that caused more bubbles to float from her mask as a mildly curious fish drifted past.

Liz and the other instructors were gesturing for the kids to follow them a little farther away from the island, and Addie saw bright pink coral spread out over the ocean floor behind them.

Unlike on dry land, Addie didn't have to make believe she was in a magical world. *Underwater, fairy tales are real,* she thought in amazement.

Addie drifted weightlessly through the water, surrounded by darting krill, hovering starfish, and seahorses that rocked gently with the current. She took a video of everything, including Jake swimming as far out as Liz would let him. He spent several minutes staring out into the dark blue, no doubt looking for sharks.

The tiniest bit of movement caught her eye, and she looked down. Beneath her flippers was a cluster of rocks.

Uh . . . I'm pretty sure one of those rocks just moved. Addie sank down lower, holding out her phone as she inspected the rock that she now realized had eyes. Delighted, Addie watched as a flatfish rose out of the sand, looking every bit like a flat smooth stone with gills as it drifted away. But it wasn't the only creature that had fooled her.

There were three dark gray rocks left, and one that was a familiar shade of blue that almost matched the rocks. Addie thought for a second her mind was playing tricks on her, and she moved closer to the blue rock, carefully filming with one hand as she reached out and tickled it with her finger.

The little penguin twisted and wiggled its way out from between the rocks, and Addie let out a delighted laugh. *Pretending to be a rock again?* she thought, moving back as the penguin soared higher. Almost as if it knew she was making a video, the penguin started to do a funny little dance, twisting and turning this way and that, putting on a show. Addie never wanted to leave the ocean, but she also couldn't wait to share this video!

She caught sight of Liz waving, and at first she thought it was time for them to go back to the surface. Then she realized Liz was pointing, and all the other kids turned to look. Addie turned, too, holding her phone out, and her breath came out in a soft whoosh when she realized what she was looking at.

Dozens of penguins were gliding toward them from all directions, coming back from their hunt. And this was nothing like watching their silly waddles on land.

It's like they magically transformed into different creatures! Addie marveled. Underwater, they soared around like graceful birds.

They seemed delighted at the presence of the scuba divers and glided around all of them in circles as the kids waved and paddled their flippers, bubbles streaming from their masks.

Addie took a video of it all, and she found her eyes were prickling with tears. Now she knew why they were called fairy penguins. Because they really did look like fairies.

But as magical as this was, she couldn't stop thinking about the foxes—and the fact that this fairy tale might not have a happily-ever-after.

17
DARWIN

Darwin zoomed up to the surface the moment he sensed the others returning from the hunt. He felt elated with himself. Yes, the girl had figured out his trick, but it had taken her a few moments! She spotted the fish before she'd realized Darwin wasn't a rock, either.

He waddled onto the beach and gave himself a shake. The rocks underwater were closer to the blue color of his feathers than the gray rocks on the island. Darwin wondered if he could bring a few of those rocks up to land. But then he realized he would have to bring enough for all the penguins in the colony to hide among them, and he felt a little deflated.

He was so lost in thought, it took him a moment to realize that Max was standing at the edge of the water, his gaze fixed on the surface.

"What's wrong?" Darwin couldn't help asking.

Max didn't move as he responded. "Is Addie okay?"

"Addie?" Darwin thought of the girl who was always with Max. "Yes, she's fine."

"But she's been under there for so long!"

Max sounded genuinely worried. Darwin waddled over to him. "She had on the mask the humans wear when they want to breathe underwater. She's having fun!"

After a moment, Max relaxed. But Darwin couldn't help thinking he looked a little bit sad.

"That's good, I want her to have fun. I just . . . Never mind," Max said. Now he finally looked at Darwin, and his eyes narrowed. "Darwin! What's rule number one?"

Darwin flicked his wings. "Stick together," he replied glumly. "But I need to have solo time! It's when I do my best thinking. And for your information, I tricked Addie! Well, almost. She thought I was a rock, for a few seconds, anyway. She kept pointing that box at me."

"It's called a *phone*." Max let out a heavy sigh. "And I told you, that's not going to work with the foxes. Not unless you can change your scent."

Darwin thought about this. "When all of us penguins are together, does that make our scent stronger?"

Max blinked. "Well, yes."

"Ha!" Darwin said triumphantly. "Then maybe it's best that we don't stick together. That will just make it easier for the foxes to smell us!"

He was pleased when Max looked dumbfounded at this. Maybe he'd outsmarted the dog. Then Max sighed again. "Darwin, I understand what you're saying, but—"

"You do? Really?" Darwin interrupted. He couldn't help it. "No one ever understands what I'm saying."

"Well, I do," Max said. "But no matter what you do to hide on this island, even if you're all alone, a fox will be able to sniff you out. Just like it will be able to sniff out the entire colony. So you have to stay together."

As if on cue, penguins began to pop out of the

water behind Darwin one at a time, their blue heads sticking up out of the waves. Tam waddled toward them, closely followed by Dubbo, Kiana, and Ferro. They lingered around Max while the other penguins passed, most of them heading to their nesting boxes.

"Hi, Max!" Tam said. "Are you here to give us more lessons?"

"Or maybe private lessons for Darwin?" Ferro added teasingly, and Kiana nudged him with her wing. She smiled at Darwin.

"I saw you in the water. That girl really thought you were a rock for a few seconds!"

Darwin raised his head proudly and looked at the others. "See? It *did* work!"

"For a few seconds," Dubbo repeated pointedly.

But Darwin was more confident than ever. "I'm going to figure this out," he told the others. "I'll show all of you!"

With that, he dove back in the water. More penguins were returning from the hunt, and the scuba divers looked ecstatic as they spun around, pointing and waving as the penguins soared all around them.

Darwin spotted Addie easily because she was still holding out that box—*phone*—and he swam right up to her. He saw her eyes widen behind her mask, and she aimed her phone at him and waved. Darwin began to twist and turn, because it was how he moved when he did his best thinking, and because he didn't care that he didn't look like the other penguins, and because maybe he wanted to show off just a little bit for Max's human.

Soon, the other scuba divers had gathered around him, too, and Max twisted and turned harder than ever. He was thinking about the last time it stormed. He was imagining Max cowering with his tail between his legs, and thinking about how the colony had all huddled together tightly against the wind as the rain lashed them, just like what Max wanted them to do if there was a fox. Darwin wasn't as afraid of storms as Max was, but he didn't exactly like them either. The winds really were rough, and the sea rose high around the island, and all the rain made it difficult to see. Plus, the thunder was a little bit frightening. And afterward, the sand was muddy and sludgy for almost an entire day, which Darwin had always found a little stinky . . .

Darwin stopped twisting and turning. He floated there in the water, aware that Addie was still holding her phone out and watching him along with all the other divers, and he wondered if they could tell that he had just had his most brilliant idea yet.

18
MAX

Max felt like he saw Addie less and less every day. They used to spend every single hour together. He would wake curled up by her feet on her bed, stick by her side as she did her homework, take walks, go fishing, have their dinner, and then curl up together at night to go to sleep.

Now, Addie was spending more and more time with friends doing things that Max couldn't do, like go to the movies. Sometimes, she would bring Max with her if she was going to hang out at Bree's or Jake's house, and Max was happy to go. But between her time with her new friends and the scuba diving, he couldn't help feeling left out.

Also, Max couldn't stop worrying about the penguins.

On Thursday, Mrs. Miller once again came over to babysit while Dad went to his trivia night. Coco and Bean came with her, but the moment Mrs. Miller stepped inside Max smelled the scent of other unfamiliar dogs.

"I adopted two new ones!" Mrs. Miller told Addie excitedly, scratching Coco on the head. "One's part sheepdog just like Max, and the other is a retriever. Their names are Molly and Tib."

"Oh, wow!" Addie exclaimed. She was on her knees, giving Coco and Bean hugs. "Why didn't you bring them, too? Max would love to meet them!"

"They're on chicken duty with the other dogs!" Mrs. Miller replied. "And those two are naturals, just like Coco and Bean here. They chased off several foxes just last night!"

Max's ears perked up at the word *fox*. He led Coco and Bean into the kitchen, where Bean immediately began drinking noisily from Max's water bowl. "The foxes tried to get the chickens last night?" Max asked Coco.

"Yes, but they didn't even get close," Coco replied. "Tib has a *very* loud bark. He scared them right off."

Max couldn't help thinking that while he was glad Mrs. Miller's chickens were safe, that could mean the foxes would redouble their efforts to try to get to the penguins.

Addie must have had the same thought as Max. "How about we visit the penguins before the sun sets? What do you think, Max?"

Max wagged his tail and gave an exuberant bark.

A few minutes later, the five of them were making their way down the beach. The tide was low enough to once again expose the path, so they walked all the way to the island.

"We can't lose track of time," Mrs. Miller pointed out, stopping to roll up the cuffs of her jeans so they wouldn't get wet. "Otherwise, we'll get stuck on the island overnight!"

Addie laughed. "That wouldn't be the worst thing."

"Speak for yourself," Mrs. Miller said. "There's a new episode of *Detective Chef* tonight!"

The penguins rushed forward to greet them as they reached the island, and Addie spent some time taking videos on her phone before leading Mrs. Miller up the slope to show off the nesting boxes she and her friends had built.

"We haven't seen the foxes in days," Tam told Max. "Do you think they've gone away?"

Max and Coco exchanged a look, and Max knew she was thinking of the den in the brush, too. "No, I don't think so. But it's okay. I'm here now." He looked around, but he didn't see Darwin among the group. Tam seemed to read his thoughts.

"Darwin was having alone time in his nesting box," she said, gesturing to the top of the slope. "His behavior has been even more unusual lately."

"And that's saying something," Dubbo added. "He's an odd one on the best of days."

"What's he doing?" Max asked.

"This morning, he kept splashing water up onto the sand and digging around in it," Dubbo told him. "I tried to ask what he was doing, and he said he was trying to change his smell. What does that even mean?"

"I think I know." Max turned to Coco and Bean. "Will you keep an eye on the pathway? I'm going to go talk to Darwin."

He left the Labs surrounded by chittering penguins and made his way up the slope. He passed
Addie and Mrs. Miller, who were cooing over a
penguin with a few eggs in one of the nesting boxes.
He didn't see Darwin anywhere, but that was
what Max's nose was for, and it didn't take long for
him to locate where Darwin was tucked away in his
nesting box.

"Found you!"

Darwin squeezed out of the opening reluctantly.
A bit of wet sand clung to his blue feathers, and he
looked disappointed. "You can still smell me? I don't
understand how! This wet sand stinks!"

"Dogs have exceptional senses of smell," Max
informed him. "So do foxes."

"You don't have to keep bragging about it,"
Darwin said.

"I'm not bragging, I'm just telling the truth," Max
informed him. "It's not like the way you smell things.
Can you smell the humans from here? Did you know
Addie and Mrs. Miller were on the island before you
came out of your nesting box?"

"Yes . . . but only because I heard their voices," Darwin admitted.

"I would be able to smell Addie even if she was on the mainland." Max turned and looked at the beach in the distance. "And I can tell the difference between all the humans' smells. Even your smell is different than the other penguins' smells. Everyone has a unique smell, but not all creatures have a good enough nose to tell the difference."

Darwin brushed some of the wet sand off his feathers. "Well, if I can't mask my smell, there has to be something else I can do to keep the colony safe from foxes!"

"I keep telling you, you can stick to the group!"

Darwin flipped his wings. "So you keep saying. We should stick together, the way we do during the storms. But that's not what you do during storms, is it? You told me you run off and hide to be alone!"

His words stung. Max hung his head a little in shame. "You're right," he admitted. And then he had an idea. "The next time there's a storm, I'm going to stick close to Addie and Dad. But only if you promise to stick with the penguins. Especially during low tide."

Darwin eyed him. "Really?"

"Really."

"Okay," Darwin said, and Max's tail flopped against the ground.

"Then you better get down there because it's low tide right now!" He nudged Darwin with his nose, and though Darwin grumbled, Max couldn't help thinking he didn't sound as put out as he normally did. He guided the little penguin down the slope—and that was when the scent of fox reached his nose.

Coco and Bean immediately began barking up a storm, running toward the edge of the island and splashing onto the path, baring their teeth. Max joined them, barking ferociously, his hackles raised. He spotted the three foxes on the beach first, and then there were another three or four emerging from the bushes.

"Remember the strategy!" Max told the penguins, and they instantly began to huddle together as tightly as possible while snapping their beaks. Max double-checked to make sure Darwin was among them. Then he turned back to face the path.

Addie and Mrs. Miller came hurrying down the slope as well. The dogs fell silent, save for the occasional growl, and everyone watched as the foxes prowled up and down the sand.

When Addie spoke, Max could hear the nervousness in her voice. "There's so many of them," she whispered. "Look, I can see a few more hiding in the brush."

"There must be a fox den," Mrs. Miller said, sounding a bit calmer. Max knew she must be used to this, always having to guard her chicken coop from predators. "They've decided to settle there because they have their eyes on the island."

Addie sounded close to tears. "I don't know what we're going to do. All it's going to take is one low tide when Max isn't here . . ."

Max let out a warning bark when one of the foxes drew too close to the path. One by one, the foxes began to retreat into the brush.

"Oh!" Addie pulled her phone out of her pocket. She turned in a slow circle, panning her phone over the penguins all huddled together, to Max and Coco and Bean, and then finally to where the foxes were prowling around on the sand.

And as she did this, she spoke in a very calm voice. "I'm visiting the penguins again before the sun sets, and I want to show you guys something that's becoming a bigger and bigger problem. During low tide, sometimes there's a path from the beach to the island, which means you can walk all the way out here. And that would be really cool, except it means other animals can get here, too. Animals like foxes. See them way out there? My dog, Max, has protected the penguins a couple of times now by scaring the foxes away. But we just realized there's a whole den of them that have made a home right there on the beach. They're just waiting for their chance to get on the island."

After the last fox had disappeared into the brush, Max looked up as Addie aimed the phone at her own face. "Max can't be here all the time, and I'm really worried about the penguins. If you guys have any ideas or suggestions, I'm all ears!"

Max turned to Coco and Bean. They stared back at him, and he could tell they were just as worried as he was. Behind them, the penguins were shaking a little bit, even Darwin. With so many foxes, Max knew there was no defense he could teach the penguins that would save them if the whole pack managed to get onto the island.

There had to be another way. And he could tell Addie was trying to figure it out. He just hoped they managed to come up with a better strategy before it was too late.

19

ADDIE

Addie and Mrs. Miller stayed on the beach with the dogs until the tide began to come in again. She uploaded the video to TikTok, and by the next morning she had hundreds of comments.

"How many views is it up to?" Dad asked, taking a big bite of toast.

"Almost ten thousand," Addie said, hardly able to believe it. She was scrolling through comment after comment, hoping for a helpful piece of advice. Everyone was lamenting about the foxes and the poor penguins and wanted to help, but no one seem to have any ideas.

Then Addie came across a comment that caused her to pause.

This account is fantastic! You're doing such a great job of raising awareness of the difficulties penguins are facing due to climate change. We love the nesting boxes! If you do come up with a plan to address this problem with the foxes, you should set up a campaign and add the link to your videos. We'd be the first to donate!

Addie saw that the account belonged to another environmental group, this one in Canada. She showed it to Dad, and he nodded thoughtfully.

"With all the attention your videos are getting, I'm sure you could get a lot of donations," he said. "I just don't know what we would do with the money."

"The only thing people are really suggesting is to get rid of the foxes," Addie said, making a face. "But they're just trying to survive, like all the other animals! It's not their fault."

She kept scrolling, but now she was barely reading the comments. That sad, desperate feeling was hitting her again, the one that always came when she thought about how much the world was changing and how little she could do about it. She remembered Mrs. Miller's words about how everyone doing just a little bit could add up to a lot. There had to be some way she could use her new TikTok following to help the penguins.

Dad cleared his throat. "So, there's something I wanted to ask you . . ."

Something in his voice made Addie look up. "Is something wrong?"

"No! No, nothing at all," Dad replied. He picked up his mug of coffee, then set it down again without taking a sip. "So tonight I have, well . . . plans. With Liz."

Addie's eyes widened. "You mean like a date?"

"No . . . well, yes," Dad admitted, and Addie started to giggle. "But I want you to be honest with me, Addie. Liz is your instructor and if this makes you uncomfortable in any way—"

"Are you kidding?" Addie exclaimed. "Dad, I've totally been trying to set you up with her!"

"You have?" Dad looked genuinely surprised. "Why?"

Addie hesitated. She didn't want to hurt Dad's feelings, but she also didn't want to lie. "It was Bree's idea," she admitted. "At first it was just because we thought that if you had a girlfriend, maybe you would let me do more stuff. Like stay home without a babysitter. And hang out with my friends without interviewing their parents first. And, well . . . Liz is the scuba-diving instructor, and I thought maybe she would be able to convince you to let me do it."

Dad crossed his arms and attempted to look stern, but Addie could tell he was amused. "Well, I guess it worked," he said. Then he sighed. "Addie, look. I know I'm a little bit overprotective. It's hard to see you grow up and go off on your own." He paused, leaning down to scratch Max between the ears. "Hard on both of us, I think."

Addie pictured Max's worried face when she went scuba diving. Suddenly, her throat felt a bit tight.

"I can't help but worry, that's all," Dad said. "When Mrs. Miller called to tell me you were missing—"

"I wasn't missing!" Addie exclaimed. "I mean, I was, but only for a few minutes. Max found me."

"Then you took that boat out to release the baby turtle—"

"And I was *fine*! Nothing bad happened!"

"My point is, you can be—"

"Impulsive, I know, I know. But Max can be impulsive, too, sometimes," Addie asserted. "He jumped off the boat to save the penguins!"

Dad smiled. "Okay, point taken. Sometimes being impulsive can be a good thing. But not always."

"Besides, that was almost a year ago," Addie pointed out. "I promise I will be the most responsible daughter on the planet if you give me a chance! Don't you trust me?"

"I do." Dad paused, drumming his fingers on the table. "So tonight, while I'm out with Liz, how about it's just you and Max."

Addie sat up straighter. "Really? No babysitter?"

"No babysitter," he replied.

Addie beamed, getting up to throw her arms around him and hugging him tightly. Then she knelt next to Max and gave him a hug as well. "Did you hear that, boy? Tonight, it's just us!"

Late that afternoon, there was another low tide. Addie walked along the beach with Dad and Max, listening as Dad went over the rules for that night for the doz-enth time.

"Where's the piece of paper with all the emergency contact numbers?" Dad asked.

Addie bent down and picked up a discarded snail crab shell. "On the fridge under the wombat magnet. But I've got you and Mrs. Miller on my phone, you know."

"And what about if you get hungry?" Dad asked.

"I can use the microwave or the oven, but not the stove," Addie said promptly. Their gas stove was a little bit temperamental, and she didn't want to use it, any-way. "As long as I can make popcorn, it's all good."

"And what about—"

"Dad!" Addie couldn't help laughing. "You're going to be gone for, what, three hours? I'm pretty sure I'll survive."

Dad slung his arm around her shoulder. "I know, I know."

Max led the way down the watery path that went to the island. It was still a few hours until sunset, but the low-hanging gray clouds made it feel even later.

"Looks like we might actually get a storm tonight," Dad said, slowing down and pulling his phone out. Addie stopped, looking at the screen as he opened the app he used to check the weather before going out to fish. Sure enough, she could see the big green splotch indicating a storm moving slowly in their direction over the ocean.

Addie felt a twinge of nerves. She didn't want Dad to use this as an excuse to cancel his date with Liz.

Dad sighed, sticking the phone back in his pocket. "You might have to deal with Max's storm anxiety," he said quietly. "Are you sure you're going to be okay, just the two of you?"

Addie nodded. "His thunder coat is in the front closet, and I'll get all his favorite toys together when we get home. We'll be fine, Dad. He'll probably just hide in my closet if it starts to thunder. It's not like he does anything crazy."

They both looked at Max at the same time. He had stopped walking as well, even though they hadn't reached the island yet. And while he wasn't growling, Addie could see immediately that something was wrong. He gazed intently at the island, one paw lifted over the wet sand, sniffing deeply. Addie stared hard at the island, and after a moment, she realized what it was.

"Where are all the penguins?" A fat drop of rain landed on Addie's cheek.

"Must be out getting dinner!" Dad said. He caught the look on Addie's face and nudged her. "It's only been low tide for a few minutes. It wasn't the foxes, Addie. The penguins are just out for another swim, that's all."

Addie nodded. She knew he was right. But there was something off about Max's stance. He took another slow, purposeful step forward, sniffing the air harder than ever. Then a low, deep rumble emitted from his chest. Addie glanced nervously at Dad. "What do you think that's about?"

Dad moved to stand next to Max, crouching down next to him. Max didn't even move. "Everything okay, boy?"

Another raindrop hit Addie's arm, and then a third.

"Oh, it's the storm!" she exclaimed. "Poor Max. He doesn't even like the rain now."

But Max wasn't acting afraid. He just looked intent.

As the raindrops began to fall a little bit faster, Dad stood up and tilted his head back to gaze at the sky. "Low tide or not, once that storm really starts, there's no way the foxes are going to be able to get through the water. We might as well head back home before we're all soaking wet!"

Addie nodded. "Come on, Max!" She and Dad took a few steps back to the mainland. For a moment, Addie thought Max was going to stay there like a statue, and her stomach gave a nervous little flip. Then in the distance, thunder rumbled long and low, and Max tucked his tail and turned around. As the rain began to fall in earnest, all three of them sprinted back toward the house.

20
DARWIN

"This way! This way! This way!"

Darwin tried his best to focus on the hunt. There was a large school of krill making its way farther and farther from the island, and the penguins had been spreading out and surrounding it slowly.

"This way!" Darwin called out, trying his best to be a part of the strategy. But he wasn't focusing as hard as he could have. His mind was still on the foxes, and the fact that he knew it would be low tide when they got back to the island. Would Max be there?

Darwin hated to admit it, but he hoped so. Huddling there with all the colony members as Max and the other dogs growled at the foxes that emerged from the bushes, Darwin had actually been frightened.

One fox was one thing, but there were almost a dozen of them. And if Max hadn't been there, Darwin knew there was no way pretending to be a rock or anything else would have worked.

"Here!"

Darwin twisted in the water and swam toward Kiana's call. Now he could see the penguins closing in from all angles on the school of krill. As he rushed toward them, he spotted another flatfish half buried in the sand, looking up at them. Darwin ignored his instinct to swim down and inspect it, and soon he reached the krill along with the rest of the colony.

He feasted along with the others, momentarily forgetting his concerns about the foxes. Then movement below caught his eye. Darwin gulped down a final krill, then drifted away from the group to inspect the ocean floor. He glided over the flat, smooth rocks, trying to spot the flatfish—because he was quite sure that was the movement he'd spotted. But this flatfish must have been exceptionally good at camouflage. Darwin couldn't spot it at all.

"Go! Go! Go!"

Darwin looked up. Far above him, the penguins were racing toward the surface. Darwin twisted and turned his way up after them. "What's going on?" he called.

Tam turned around and spotted him. "Darwin, *hurry! Sea lions!*"

Alarmed, Darwin looked around. After a moment, he spotted the dark shapes of the sea lions. They were a good distance away, but every penguin knew how quickly a sea lion could move.

Darwin sped after the others to the surface, where fat, cold drops of rain immediately began to hit his head. He waddled up onto the coast along with the rest of the penguins.

"Why did you go off on your own?" Tam chided him. "That was dangerous, Darwin! You have to stick to the group!"

Darwin didn't respond. There was no point in explaining about the flatfish—he'd already tried, and no one understood. Instead, he waddled over to the shore that faced the mainland.

There was still a little light outside, although the

clouds overhead were thick and dark. Kiana joined him, and they stared out at the path. Or rather, where the path would be.

"It's not there," said Darwin, relieved.

"I guess the coast can't eat the sea when it's raining," Kiana said.

Darwin was pleased that she'd used his phrase. But he still felt uneasy. There was no way the foxes could reach them if the path wasn't exposed, but something felt . . . off.

As the wind began to pick up and thunder rumbled in the distance, the penguins automatically huddled together in the center of the island. As usual, Darwin tuned out the chittering and chattering. After the hunt, he was longing for a little solo time. He wondered if Max was keeping to his word right now and sticking close to Addie.

"Something strange is happening," Tam said suddenly, and Darwin twisted around to look at her.

The other penguins fell silent, a ripple of unease going through the group. Now that they were all still, Darwin's senses prickled. He knew exactly what words he wanted to use. But he didn't want to say the words because he knew no one would understand him.

"Does anyone see the foxes?" Ferro asked. The penguins all turned to gaze hard at the mainland. Through the rain, Darwin could see the brush, but it was still. There was not a sign of red anywhere. He so wanted to say the words his mind was shouting, but they wouldn't understand . . . would they?

"There's no sign of them," Dubbo said. "They'll probably stay in their den since it's raining."

"Yes, but it just feels like . . ." Tam trailed off. "I don't know. Like they're watching."

"Watching. Watching. Watching."

Darwin listened to the word ripple around the colony. He understood what they meant. And finally, he couldn't stop himself from saying it.

"The foxes are invisible."

"Invisible? Invisible? Invisible?"

The word rippled around the colony, but no one teased him. For a moment, there was silence. Then Kiana said, "Darwin is right. That's exactly what it feels like. Like the foxes are watching us, but we can't watch them."

Darwin couldn't believe it. Not one of the penguins, not even Ferro, made fun of him. Instead, they all huddled together even more tightly. As thunder rumbled again, Darwin couldn't help but think about Max.

"Should we get back in the water?" Kiana asked nervously.

"We can't," Tam pointed out. "The sea lions are much too close to the island. We're safer on the island."

Are we? Darwin wondered. But he kept the thought to himself.

After a while, when nothing happened, the penguins started chatting away. The urge to be alone was too great, and besides, Darwin wanted to figure out what was going on. He quietly waddled away from the group when no one was looking and began to make his way up the slope. They couldn't see the foxes down there, but maybe from a higher vantage point, he could figure out where they were.

He just wanted to see them on the mainland. Then, Darwin would feel safe.

21
MAX

Max and Addie were curled up on the sofa with a big bowl of popcorn. Addie was watching a movie and texting with her friends, tossing a piece of popcorn to Max every few minutes. She had her feet tucked underneath his stomach and, every once in a while, she would wiggle her toes and tickle him.

It should have been relaxing. But Max was anything but relaxed.

The rain pattered gently against the window, but that wasn't the reason Max was on edge. He knew the storm was going to get worse, he could see that Addie had laid out the big heavy coat she and Dad would strap him into when the thunder got really bad. Having that heavy weight on his back did help make him feel somewhat better. But Max was on edge for another reason.

When they'd been walking to Penguin Island, the smell of fox had been *everywhere*.

If Max hadn't known any better, he would have thought the foxes were lurking around them in the water. He'd been relieved to see the penguins were all out hunting, and when they turned around and headed back to the beach, Max had looked back to see that the path was already disappearing beneath the water. The foxes were nearby, there was no doubt about that. But if there was one good thing about the storm, it was that even during low tide, the penguins would be protected.

Still, Max couldn't shake the feeling that he was missing something.

"Oh, Mrs. Miller just texted me a video of her new pups!" Addie held out her phone in front of Max's nose. On the screen, Coco and Bean were racing around Mrs. Miller's yard with a young sheepdog and a golden retriever. The rain pounded the windows a little bit harder, and Max whimpered.

"It's okay, boy," Addie said, shifting closer to him and resting her arm along his back. "I can't wait to meet Mrs. Miller's new dogs. Maybe we could talk Dad into getting you a brother or sister! Jake keeps saying the shelter is way too crowded, there are lots of dogs that need . . ."

Addie trailed off, and then there was another low, distant rumble of thunder. Max tucked his tail between his legs as he stiffened, but he remembered his promise to Darwin and stayed put right there on the couch. The storm was coming in over the ocean; he could feel it in the wind that had been blowing over the water earlier.

Max's head jerked up. That was what was bothering him! Wind carried smells with it. And this wind was coming from the ocean, not the mainland.

So why did it smell so strongly of fox?

"Max, I just had an amazing idea!" Addie sat up straight, removing her arm from his back, her thumbs flying over her screen. "Operation Save the Penguins, Part Two. I really think this might work."

Addie continued to ramble, but Max wasn't trying

to pick out any of the words anymore. His hackles were raised, and he couldn't stop picturing the empty island. The penguins were probably returning from the hunt by now, and he could picture them all huddling together tightly in a group to face the storm, just like Darwin said. Only now that they had the nesting boxes, maybe they would take shelter there, waddling up the slope and—

BOOM!

Thunder seemed to rattle the walls of the house, but that wasn't why Max leaped off the couch.

"Max, no!" Addie cried, jumping up and throwing her phone aside. "It's okay, it's just thunder!"

But thunder had nothing to do with it. The penguins were in terrible danger, Max just knew it. He bolted straight for the door, ignoring Addie's cries and slipping through the doggie door.

Max ran down the beach, straight into the storm.

22

ADDIE

"Max!"

Addie threw the front door open and ran after him, her heart pounding frantically against her chest. "Max! *Stop!*"

She ran as fast as she could, but Max was tearing full speed down the beach. The rain was coming down in sheets now, and within seconds, Addie was soaked from head to toe. Her mind was working over-time, trying to figure out what was going on. Max always ran to hide in her closet during a storm. It didn't make any sense that he would run outside right *into* the storm!

"Max!" she screamed one more time, but it was lost to another clap of thunder. She could see Max plowing into the water now. The tide wasn't completely high, but the water was choppy thanks to the storm. Addie slowed to a stop as she watched Max begin to swim straight toward Penguin Island.

Addie pushed her wet hair off her face and looked around frantically. Max wouldn't be doing this unless he thought the penguins were in danger, but she couldn't see foxes anywhere. There was no way they could make it to the island with the water this high, especially during a storm!

Her eyes fell on the rowboat tied up near the dock, and she took two steps toward it. Then she remembered her promise to Dad about how she wouldn't be impulsive this time. But she'd left her phone inside, and Max was in the water . . .

Addie's thoughts whirled like a hurricane in her head. Going out into the ocean in a rowboat to release a baby turtle was one thing. But doing it at night, during a storm? *That* was definitely not a good idea.

Addie stared hard at the island. She thought she could make out the penguins all huddled together as Max made his way toward them. Nothing was wrong as far as she could see, but Addie trusted Max's instincts. Something was wrong. This was definitely an emergency.

But if she got in that rowboat, it might turn into an even *bigger* emergency.

Fighting the almost overwhelming urge to follow Max, Addie turned around and sprinted back to the house.

23
DARWIN

The foxes are invisible.

Darwin stopped waddling. He was only a little bit of the way up the hill, his eyes on the top of the slope. He just wanted to crawl into his nesting box for some solo time.

But something was telling him to stop.

He stared at the closest nesting box. The entrance was dark, and he was so tempted to crawl right inside, moving around the tunnel and into the cozy space where he would be protected from the wind and the rain. But there was something off about it. As he stared, he saw something shift in the darkness of the tunnel.

The truth hit Darwin like a mighty wave.

Turning, he waddled back down the slope and toward the colony as fast as his feet could carry him.

"The foxes are being penguins!"

At first, no one heard him above all the chittering, then one by one the penguins all fell silent and listened. Then they began to repeat Darwin's words.

"Foxes being penguins! Foxes being penguins! Foxes being penguins!"

Darwin came face-to-face with Tam. "The foxes are being penguins in the nesting boxes!"

She stared hard at him, and Darwin could see a little flash of fear in her eyes.

"The foxes can't fit in the nesting boxes," she said.

Darwin twisted and turned, even though he wasn't in the water. "They're in the tunnels! They're curled up tight inside, waiting for us!"

He tried to stay still, waiting for Tam to dismiss him or for Ferro to make fun of him. But then, to his astonishment, Tam tilted her head.

"Something has felt off ever since we returned from the hunt," she said. "Darwin is right, everyone. The foxes are here. They must've snuck onto the island while we were out hunting and the path was exposed."

For a moment, Darwin forgot his fear. Tam understood! She believed him!

"What do we do?" Dubbo asked.

Darwin was amazed to find that everyone was looking at him. Even Tam! He thought of what Max had said.

"Foxes use their noses to find us," he told everyone. "But mud might cover up our scent. Everyone roll around in the mud!"

He flopped down in the mud and began to roll around. Kiana, Ferro, and several other penguins did the same. But then Tam let out a cry. "They're coming down the hill! Back in the water!"

Darwin looked up. All over the slope, the foxes were creeping out of the nesting boxes and moving fast toward the penguins. Three moved swiftly around to the left, while four more moved to the right, and soon the penguins were between the foxes and the water.

"What do we do?" Kiana fretted.

"Head for the water!" Ferro yelled.

"No, the sea lions are too close!" Dubbo cried.

"Huddle together! Snap your beaks!" Tam commanded, and the penguins did as they were told. Darwin was packed in between Ferro and Dubbo, but for once he didn't mind.

He definitely did not want solo time right now.

As the foxes closed in on them, Darwin and his friends braced themselves for a fight. Then there was a splashing sound behind them followed by a mighty bark.

"Max!"

24
MAX

Max's thick coat was heavy with rain and seawater, but he paddled as hard as he could toward the island. Lightning flashed, briefly lighting up the sky, framing the penguins all huddled together.

And they weren't alone.

The foxes were creeping out of the nesting boxes and making their way down the slope.

The penguins squeezed tighter, snapping their beaks just like he'd taught them.

Max barked once, loudly and sharply, and a wave slapped him in the mouth. But it was enough to make the foxes freeze for a moment.

Max sped up, paddling even harder against the waves until at last his paws found the rocky coast.

He lunged forward, and the penguins parted as he moved straight through the group and stood in front of them, planting his paws and baring his teeth. Lightning flashed again, followed by the loudest clap of thunder yet.

BOOM!

But Max didn't run. He didn't tuck his tail between his legs. He stayed there, growling and staring down at least one dozen foxes.

"Stay together!" he called to the penguins, and they obediently clustered close behind him. "Snap your beaks!"

He heard them *snap-snap-snapping.* But the foxes still didn't move. Max could tell they were sizing him up, weighing their odds. He couldn't fight a dozen foxes at once. If a few of them tousled with Max, the others would be free to go after the penguins. But he could tell none of them wanted to be the ones to fight him.

Another flash of lightning, and then—*BOOM!*

One of the foxes took a step back, and so did another. Max intensified his growling. Next to him, Tam moved closer.

"Thank goodness you're here! We didn't realize the foxes were on the island when we came back from our hunt."

"Thank goodness for Darwin," Dubbo added. "He's the one who realized where the foxes were hiding."

Max tore his eyes off the foxes briefly. "Darwin? Where is he?" For a moment, he had a horrible thought that Darwin had waddled off on his own again to the nesting boxes and discovered the foxes for himself. Then Darwin appeared on his other side.

"Right here, just like I promised," Darwin said. "And you don't look afraid of storms to me!"

Max felt a wave of relief as he faced the foxes again. They were still moving backward step-by-step up the slope, their eyes fixed on the penguins.

"Max, afraid of storms?" Tam said. "I don't think Max is afraid of anything!"

And in that moment, Max realized she was right. He was standing on an island in the middle of a raging thunderstorm, facing down the foxes. He wasn't afraid at all.

He huddled there with the penguins for what felt

like an endless standoff. The foxes remained on the slope—they didn't come any closer, but they also didn't retreat into the nesting boxes. Finally, Max heard a ripple go through the penguins, one word: *"Boat! Boat! Boat!"*

Max didn't turn back to look, but the wind carried a scent he recognized instantly.

Addie.

The rain poured down and the thunder boomed, but Max didn't flinch. Addie was coming, and so was Dad.

With his family at his side, Max could face anything.

25
ADDIE

The last half hour had been the longest of Addie's life as she waited for Dad to come home. At least a hundred different scenarios of what could be happening on Penguin Island had played out in her mind—and not one of them had a happily-ever-after.

When Dad's truck had finally come rumbling down the road, Addie sprinted outside to greet him.

"Hurry!" she cried as Dad and Liz leaped out of the truck. The three of them raced through the pouring rain down the beach. Without a word, Addie began pushing the rowboat toward the shore. Liz and Dad helped, but before they reached the water—

"ARF-ARF-ARF-ARF!"

"Max!" Addie screamed, her heart leaping into her

throat. She had never, *ever* heard Max bark like that. It sounded almost like an alarm.

She squinted, trying to see through the sheets of rain. The penguins were huddled around Max, who was facing the slope. At first, Addie couldn't tell what he was looking at. Then lightning lit up the sky, and Addie let out a cry of shock.

"The foxes!"

At least a dozen foxes were on the slope, and one by one, they were moving toward the penguins—and Max.

Desperately, Addie shoved the rowboat again. But then Liz cried, "Tim! What are you doing?"

Addie looked up to see Dad *running straight into the water!*

"Shoo! *Get back!*" Dad yelled, waving his hands over his head. Instantly, every single fox went still as their focus shifted from Max to Dad. Addie stood there with her mouth hanging open as Dad ran, then swam, then climbed up onto the shore. The foxes began retreating up the slope, and the knot in Addie's stomach loosened slightly.

She turned to Liz, who looked just as shocked as she felt. "Let's get this boat out there," Liz said finally, and Addie nodded.

Together, they shoved the boat out onto the water until the current picked it up. Liz climbed in first, then helped Addie on board.

When they reached Penguin Island, Addie clambered out of the boat and raced over to Max, slinging both arms around him. He was sopping wet, and he kept his eyes locked on the slope.

"You're a hero," Addie whispered. *"Again."*

BOOM!

Addie flinched, waiting for Max to leap out of her arms. But he just leaned into Addie a little bit, and his tail thumped once, twice, three times on the rocky ground. She planted a kiss on his soggy head, then stood up as Dad and Liz joined them.

"You *ran* to the island in the middle of a *storm*," Addie said to Dad, still unable to believe it. "That was pretty impulsive, Dad."

Dad let out a little laugh. "I guess it was. But I wasn't about to let Max here face down the foxes alone."

"I don't understand," Liz said as Addie got to her feet and pulled out her phone. "How did the foxes get out here in the storm in the first place?"

Addie aimed her phone at the slope, taking a video as the foxes slipped into the nesting boxes. "I don't think they got here during the storm," she said slowly. "I think they snuck onto the island *before* the storm and hid in the nesting boxes."

"Oh, my goodness," Liz breathed. "I think you're right."

"They're crafty creatures," Dad said, shaking his head. "This was a close call."

Addie filmed the penguins, all huddled around Max. Right before he'd raced out into the storm, Addie had been looking at photos of Mrs. Miller's new puppies she'd adopted from the shelter, and a wild idea had started to form in her mind.

But maybe it wasn't so wild after all . . .

Hours later, Addie sat cross-legged in front of a roaring fire, her hands wrapped around a mug of hot cocoa. Max was curled up at her side, fur still slightly damp despite her and Dad's best efforts to dry him off.

Dad and Liz sat side by side on the sofa holding steaming cups of ginger tea. They were still deep in discussion about what had happened—or rather, what had *almost* happened. Once again, Max had saved the penguins. Thanks to Addie's waterproof case, she'd captured it all on video: the penguins huddling behind Max when the rain and tide subsided, the foxes slinking off the island back to the mainland, and Dad and Liz double-checking every last nesting box to make sure the penguins were safe.

She hadn't uploaded the videos to TikTok—not yet. Addie knew they would get a ton of attention.

But she wanted more than just lots of views. She wanted to use her new platform to actually make a difference.

"Dad? Liz?"

They looked up. "Yes, hon?" Dad asked.

Addie took a deep breath. "Jake's been talking about how the animal shelter is really overcrowded. Mrs. Miller, too—she just adopted a couple puppies, and she's going to train them to guard the chickens like Coco and Bean do. And that made me think . . . what if we train the dogs who haven't been adopted yet to guard the penguins, like Max does?"

Neither Dad nor Liz spoke, and Addie felt a little flutter of doubt. But she ignored it and continued.

"I got a comment on one of my TikTok videos about taking donations to help the penguins," she told them, rubbing Max behind the ear as she spoke. "If I put a link in all my videos, I might be able to raise enough money to start some sort of organization that trains shelter dogs to be, I don't know, like penguin guardians. There could be a schedule where the dogs all take turns being out on the island. It would be fun for the dogs, being outside instead of in a kennel. And Max could teach them, the way he helps train puppies when we go to the dog park, and . . ." She trailed off, looking at Dad. "You think it's a bad idea?"

Dad blinked. "Honey, I think it's a *brilliant* idea."

Addie's face grew warm. "Really?"

"Really."

"Penguin Guardians!" Liz exclaimed. "That's the name you should go with. It's perfect!"

"Agreed," Dad said proudly. "So you're going to start taking donations?"

Addie glanced down at her phone. She was longing to share those videos and start asking for donations right this very second . . . but that would be impulsive. And Addie didn't want to mess this up.

She smiled at Dad. "First, I think we need to come up with a strategy."

Epilogue

"Max! Ready for school?"

Addie clapped her hands once. Max woke with a start from his nap, stretching his limbs.

"Come on, lazybones," Addie said, holding out a blue vest with the words PENGUIN GUARDIANS: TEACHER printed along the side. "Time to get dressed!"

Addie clasped the buckles under Max's belly, then made sure the vest was straight. She couldn't help checking her phone again, even though she had checked it just after breakfast.

After the incident with the foxes two months ago, Addie's videos of the whole event had gone viral. The response had been overwhelming, but in the best possible way. News outlets all over the world had shared Addie's video of Max swimming through a storm and saving the penguins from the foxes. The last time she looked, it had over a million views.

She'd had to turn off TikTok notifications because her phone was chiming nonstop!

And Addie had taken that one commenter's advice and added a link to an account where people could make donations for Operation Save the Penguins. It seemed like everyone from New York to Tokyo to Berlin was now aware of the plight of the fairy penguins, and they all wanted to do their part to help.

Addie, Max, and Dad set off down the beach together. It was low tide today, and there were lots more people than usual milling back and forth on the path between the beach and the island.

"Addie! Over here!"

Jake waved both arms over his head, then made the scuba signal for *distress*. Addie and Dad laughed as at least a dozen dogs swarmed around him, gobbling up the crisps that had fallen out of his pocket. Bree was nearby, strapping a German shepherd into a blue harness that said PENGUIN GUARDIANS: STUDENT.

Max bounded over to Jake, who immediately pulled more crisps from his pocket. Addie waved at Mrs. Miller, who was chatting with the animal shelter director while

Coco and Bean sat obediently at her feet. They both wore TEACHER harnesses, like Max.

With Dad's help, Addie had completed all the paperwork to start a nonprofit organization last month. The mission of Penguin Guardians was simple: train dogs from the animal shelter to guard the blue penguins. Once a dog completed training, he would become a teacher like Max. That way, there would always be a few dogs on Penguin Island during low tide. Jake had introduced Addie to the director of the animal shelter, and they partnered with Addie's organization so that each low tide was also an adoption event! People could come out to meet all the dogs who needed a home.

And, of course, the hundreds of fairy penguins whose home was safe once again.

"What a great turnout!" Liz joined them, slipping her hand into Dad's. "I hope you're taking tons of videos."

"Of course!" Addie said, waving her phone.

Max's first lesson with the dogs was a blast. Addie watched proudly as he helped the dogs get to know the penguins, who were chitter-chattering nonstop. After the storm, Addie, Dad, and Liz had stayed on the island with Max and the penguins until, at last, the rain had let up and the foxes had slunk around them and sprinted back to the mainland. They hadn't been spotted since—Mrs. Miller had even brought Coco and Bean over to sniff around and confirm that their den was gone. The foxes had moved on. And thanks to Max and the other dogs, they wouldn't see the penguins as such an easy target anymore.

When Max broke away from the pack, sniffing the ground intently, Addie followed him with her phone. He snuffled and sniffed his way up the slope until he reached a patch of weeds and what *almost* looked like three rocks. Then he let out a short bark.

Addie giggled as the three penguins all leaped up and shook the mud off their feathers. Two of them scuttled away, but the littlest penguin lingered by Max. Bree and Jake joined Addie as she knelt to take a close-up video of the penguin.

"I swear, I think they were playing hide-and-seek

with Max!" she told them. The littlest penguin waddled away, moving all the way up the slope and diving into the water. Addie hoped he wouldn't be too tired later this afternoon during her scuba-diving lesson. The littlest penguin was a total camera hog! He was definitely the star of her TikTok account. Well, aside from Max.

Addie watched as Max trotted back over to the colony and his eager students. More people were gathering on the beach, and Addie saw several people waiting to talk to the animal shelter director. A man and his young daughter seemed interested in the German shepherd—they were laughing with delight as Jake led the puppy through a few basic commands. Bree was carrying a clipboard as she wandered around, asking kids if they'd like to sign up for Eco-Guardians. Two little girls raced up the path toward the island, giggling with glee as the water splashed around their ankles. They made a beeline for Bree, begging to sign up.

The path between Penguin Island and the mainland still looked strange to Addie, a reminder that the world was changing in ways that felt overwhelming. But everyone here was doing their part to help.

And lots of people doing a little bit to help could add up to *big* change. Like giving the fairy penguins a happily-ever-after.

ACKNOWLEDGMENTS

Thank you as always to my wonderful editor, Orlando Dos Reis, to Chelsea Eberly at Greenhouse Literary Agency, and to everyone at Scholastic, including Omou Barry, Amanda Maciel, Mary Kate Garmire, Priscilla Eakeley, Lori Lewis, Jael Fogle, Adriann Ranta Zurhellen, and Cady Zeng.

Special thanks to Rosa, my own little polar bear who would probably be terrified of a penguin if she met one, and to Josh, who encourages me to have new adventures. And a big thank-you to my foster doggo, Buddy, who provided inspiration for Max's storm anxiety and got his own happily-ever-after in his forever home!

ABOUT THE AUTHOR

Michelle Schusterman is the author of over twenty books for kids and teens, including *The Dog's Meow*, *Some Bunny to Love*, and *My Otter Half*. She documents her writing process and journey as an author on her YouTube channel, and she can be found roaming the coast and searching in vain for penguins with her husband, Josh, and their Lab, Rosa.